T.D. and the TATER

And Other News from Augusta County

Sam Adams

Bodmin Books Ltd. Co.

T.D. AND THE TATER
AND OTHER NEWS FROM AUGUSTA COUNTY

A Bodmin Book

First Edition/May 2011

ISBN: 0615455859
ISBN-13: 978-0615455853
Library of Congress Control Number: 2011903345

PRINTED IN THE UNITED STATES OF AMERICA
10 9 8 7 6 5 4 3 2 1

Inquiries to:
Bodmin Books Ltd. Co.
P.O. Box 326
Whitesburg, KY 41858
rights@bodminbooksltd.com

AND IN OTHER NEWS...

Roger Shepherd's exploits with the "cobra" had been traveling the gossip circuit for three weeks when a greasy-haired man in a white t-shirt, dirty blue jeans, and knee-high boots came into the office. I'd seen boots like those before.

"Are you the Pitcher Man?" he asked.

I knew immediately that this was my big chance, and I'd better take it.

"Sorry," I said, stepping around the man and going out the door. "He's gone to lunch."

T.D. and the TATER

And Other News from Augusta County

PART ONE

T.D. AND THE TATER

S ometimes it doesn't take much to be a small-town hero.

It takes giving the district champ basketball team a ride on the fire truck, or being the only cop in town and changing a flat for the Sunday school teacher. Mostly, it happens purely by chance.

My chance walked in the door at five minutes 'til lunch one sunny August morning.

Clarence Baker shuffled into *The Wakefield Journal* office three months after I graduated from college and came home to Augusta County. I was pretty sure I knew the type, but, against my better judgment, I asked him if I could help him.

He was about fifty-five and obviously spent most of his time toiling away in a field somewhere or other. His gray hair stuck out from under a Tractor Supply hat and the sun had turned the back of his neck and the lower half of his arms to cordovan leather. He polished his glasses on the tail of his work uniform shirt and shifted his weight from one mud-covered brogan to the other.

"Are you the Pitcher Man?" he asked.

I like to think of myself as a journalist, but to the people in Augusta County, I was "that reporter feller," or simply "son-of-a-bitch." Given the last alternative, I was perfectly happy to answer to "Pitcher Man."

"I'm T.D. Duff," I nodded.

Clarence looked at me blankly for a moment, and then stuck out his hand. "Pleased to meet ya. I'm Clarence Baker," he said, pronouncing his first name with only a single syllable. "Is the Pitcher Man here?"

"Yes. That's me. Sorry." I regretted the conversation already.

Clarence nearly jumped in the air with excitement.

"I've got a pitcher I want to put in the paper."

"Have you got it with you?"

Again the blank stare. "Got what with me?"

I wasn't sure if he was putting me on or not. "The picture," I reminded him.

"Oh, I ain't got no pitcher. I want you to take a pitcher!"

"Oh!" I said, suddenly understanding. "What of?"

"It's somethin' unlike anything you've ever seen in your whole entire life."

I nodded expectantly and waited.

"Well? What is it?"

Clarence gave me the self-assured grin of a carnival huckster drawing his prey into the sideshow.

"It's a tater."

It was my turn to look blank.

"A tater?"

"Gotcha, didn't I?" Clarence laughed. "It ain't just any tater; it's special."

"A special tater. I see." I dutifully scribbled in my notebook as I tried to think of something—anything—to say that wouldn't sound like I was making fun of this poor man. "So, what's special about it?"

"Come outside and I'll show ya." Clarence turned on ball-bearing soles and hurried out the door.

I followed him outside and around to the tailgate of a blue-and-rust Chevy pickup. Clarence motioned for me to stand back then lowered the tailgate and made a gesture that would have made the models on *The Price Is Right* proud.

"Ta-da!"

I gazed at the brown tuber in the back of the truck and tried not to look dumbfounded.

"Goddawg! That's a ... a ... nice potato," I said. "It's a <u>big</u> potato."

Clarence looked at me like I was crazy. "You ain't from around here, are you? I've got hun'erts of 'em bigger than that. Can't you see it?"

I shrugged my shoulders and struggled for an answer. "I <u>am</u> from around here, but..."

"Let me hold it up the right way." He turned the potato so the narrow end pointed down and beamed at me.

"Who does that look like now?"

"Mr. Potatohead?"

Clarence laughed. "You're joshin' me. You're a smart feller. You watch T.V., don't you?"

"Well, sure, I watch T.V."

"Well, look at it. It looks just like him!"

"Well, yeah, I guess it does, now that you mention it," I said, hopefully waiting for Clarence to tell me who "him" was.

Clarence was beginning to catch on and he looked hurt.

"Can't you see it? Here. Let me turn it to the sun so you can get a better look. See?"

"I'm sorry, Clarence. Maybe if you told me, I could see the resemblance."

Clarence looked at me with disgust.

"Magnum!"

I must have looked blank again because Clarence certainly looked disgusted again.

"Magnum, P.I.," he explained. "I thought you said you watch T.V."

"I do, I do," I said hurriedly. "I guess the sun was just too bright."

Clarence wasn't sure I saw it yet.

"You do think it looks like him, don't ya?"

"Well, yeah. A little around the eyes."

Clarence grinned triumphantly. "You put this on the front page of your paper and you'll have to print extra copies this week. Everybody in Augusta County'll be talkin' about me and my tater."

"I bet you're right." I took the lens cap off my Pentax and snapped a picture. Clarence yanked off his glasses and stuck them in his pocket, posing proudly with the Irish potato. That week was slow so Bug Wake, the publisher, put the potato on the front page with a caption that said, "Stars in his eyes."

It was good for a laugh, but for me it was over. At least I thought it was over. Suddenly I became the man who could make you famous in Augusta County. It was as though I were casting director for *Magnum, P.I.* People lined up outside *The Journal* door, radishes and rutabagas in hand. Bug was kept busy hanging framed still-lives of vegetables in the lobby.

I had become the go-to guy for green beans. The potentate of potatoes. The top tomato in Augusta County. I couldn't go to the grocery store without the produce man shaking my hand and pointing out how much the cantaloupes reminded him of Dolly Parton.

I was a local hero. And I planned to parlay that fame into real, honest-to-goodness news-gathering ability. And a potato was at the root of it all.

"Theodore, you're not eating your turnips," Mama said, as she nibbled on Humphrey Bogart's ear.

We sat in the dining room of my childhood home, the table spread with all manner of garden vegetables, each reminding me of a living, breathing human being. Or at least a formerly living one.

"Sorry, Mama. They just remind me too much of … you know."

"Don't be silly. Humphrey Bogart was much better looking than a turnip. Besides, he had that angular face—more like a parsnip, if you ask me."

She took a bite of "Bean" Crosby and my stomach turned.

"I can't, Mama. Really. I think I'll go to the dairy bar and eat in the car after it gets dark."

"You'll get a stomachache," Mama said, taking another bite of Bogey. "Surely we have something you can eat."

I started to shake my head until I saw the fruit basket at the other end of the table.

"On second thought, maybe I'll just have a cantaloupe or two."

Bug was watching a ballgame and smoking a cigar at the office when I stopped by to pick up some film to keep in the car.

"What are you doing back?" he asked. "I thought you went to dinner at your mom's house."

"I did. We're finished already."

"How was it?"

"It was a bust."

"I know what you mean. My mother never could cook worth a damn, either."

"Well. I gotta go," I said, starting for the door.

"Hey, T.D.?"

"Yeah?"

"I hope you didn't get that film so you could take more vegetable pictures. The cattle farmers are startin' to get jealous."

"Well, Mrs. Fisher over at Bear Fork did call to say she had a cabbage head that looks like Henry Kissinger."

"Catherine Fisher?"

"Yeah, why?"

"She hasn't paid her subscription bill in two years. I've been meaning to cut her off; I just haven't gotten around to it. Tell her we charge fifty-two dollars to take a picture. If she pays, you can take the picture. But she has to pay in advance. That old biddy would steal the nickels off a dead man's eyes. She's been that way ever since before the war."

"World War II?"

"No, the Civil War."

"Did you know her back then?" I smirked behind Bug's recliner.

"No, but she was my first-grade teacher in 1922," Bug answered. "Now, do like I told you. If she'll pay you, I'll even let you keep five bucks as a commission."

"Only five bucks?"

"It's only two years."

The fifty-two-dollar fee was so steep that Henry Kissinger never made the paper and I never earned the five-dollar commission. However, I did earn the nickname "son-of-a-bitch" when I told Mrs. Fisher I had to charge her for the photo.

The number of celebrity vegetables started to slack off, but the folks who had been lucky enough to have a star in the garden were so grateful for the fame that I didn't have to buy produce all that fall. They kept me supplied with everything I could ever want. My appetite eventually returned, and I was able to eat the offerings without feeling like a cannibal.

Another benefit was that the farmers trusted me completely, and called whenever they thought something was newsworthy. I was enjoying a flood of news tips, and the expectations of the tipsters kept Bug from butchering the stories too badly.

I had nearly forgotten about Clarence Baker until he called me on the phone in mid-November with another revelation. Magnum, P.I. was going to be in the homecoming parade.

"You're kidding," I said. "I can't believe somebody actually got a star like that to come here."

"Oh, I don't mean the real Magnum, P.I. I mean his look-alike."

"You mean the tater?"

"Yep. The Augusta High Class of 1968 asked me and Magnum to ride on their float and be grand marshals."

"I can't believe you've still got Magnum. What's it been now, three or four months since you dug him up?"

"That ain't old for a tater," Clarence said. "You know how everybody that raises a garden has a tater hole or a cellar to keep them over the winter? I dug him his own private hole in the backyard and I tuck him in every night. Besides, I shellacked him so he'd keep better. He ain't even had a single sprout."

"That's great," I said, laying my forehead on the desk.

"Anyhow, just wanted to make sure you knew about it. I knew you'd want to take another pitcher."

"Thanks, Clarence. I wouldn't miss it for the world."

I hung up and tried to think of a way to avoid the potato parade. I was just formulating a plan when Bug walked in with the morning mail.

"I got a hot one for you, T.D. The Augusta High Homecoming Committee sent us a news release. Magnum, P.I. is gonna be the grand marshal of the parade."

"It's the potato, Bug, not the T.V. star," I said.

"I know. Isn't it great?"

"Great? It's a potato."

"But it's local. That's where the interest is," Bug said. "Who cares if some hotshot movie star rides through town for thirty minutes? But a local boy— that's a different story."

"It's a local root crop."

"It's still local. That's the key word: local."

"Bug, that's the same day as the food drive at the theater," I said. "They advertise, so I thought we should cover what they're doing."

"Advertise, smadvertise. It's a ten-dollar ad and nobody'll go see their movies if they don't run it. Besides, you can always take a picture of a can of green beans. A real live tater is a once-in-a-lifetime opportunity."

The big day finally arrived. The parade lined up for two miles down the highway, led by fire trucks and ambulances. The floats—mostly pickup trucks and farm tractors with hay trailers behind—were next in line, followed by tricked-out tractor-trailers and a cadre of motorbikes and ATVs. Danny Vaughn, owner of the Augusta Funeral Home and my best friend in the world, waved from a horse-drawn hearse.

The horses, for obvious reasons, usually pulled up to the rear. This year, however, the homecoming committee was particularly irked at the Wakefield Middle School PTO for failing to come up with their share of the money for the giant homecoming cake, and they put the marching band from that school immediately behind the Arabians and Appaloosas.

I spent thirty minutes before the starting siren walking up and down beside the parade lineup, snapping pictures of pretty cheerleaders, tough-looking football players, and sixty-year-old men trying to keep the buttons on their old letterman sweaters from popping.

I found Clarence between a new fire tanker and a Corvette carrying Carolina Cole, the six-year-old winner of the Little Miss Pumpkin beauty pageant. She was dressed in a bright orange evening gown and had on a little too much makeup, but other than that she was a beautiful little girl. The eye shadow even made her look a little like a jack-o-lantern.

Clarence and Magnum looked splendid, too. Clarence had slicked down what little gray hair he had left and polished his brogans 'til they almost shined. He was wearing sparkling clean work pants and a polyester Hawaiian shirt. A rubber band kept the sole of his right shoe from flapping up and down. He sat on top of a volcano made out of wood and chicken wire covered in wads of tissue paper spray-painted brown. I overheard a group of cattle farmers trying to figure out where anybody got a cow flop that big, and where they got a volcano to set it on.

No matter what the float looked like, Magnum P.I. was positively regal. Clarence had perched a red velour pillow with yellow tassels on the corners at the very peak of the volcano, and Magnum reposed in the center of the pillow, his skin glistening with shellac. Clarence had even found a little Detroit Tigers cap for him. I can't swear to it, but it kinda looked like he had painted a Mr. Potatohead accessory.

"Are you ready for this, Clarence?" I hollered.

"I was born ready," Clarence hollered back. "Magnum's a little nervous, though. He ain't never been in front of a crowd this big."

"Well, that's the price of stardom. Let me go ahead and take your picture now in case it gets too dark later."

"You're the Pitcher Man," Clarence replied, putting his arm around the back of Magnum's pillow and showing me his new dentures.

I snapped a couple of shots and then said goodbye to Clarence and Magnum. I found a spot on the judges' stand and waited for the parade to begin. When the volcano float came in sight, Clarence was grinning like…well, a crazy man and waving both hands at the crowd. Magnum was just sort of sitting there.

They got right in front of the judges' stand when the driver of the pickup pulling the float green-horned the clutch. The resulting jerk caused Magnum to roll over backward and tumble down the volcano. Clarence made a desperate grab as the potato made the slow-motion fall onto the steel trailer floor and shattered into a thousand putrid pieces.

Magnum may have not been that old for a potato, but he was rotten to the core. The Class of '68, all dressed in Hawaiian shirts and grass skirts, scrambled to get away from the noxious fumes. Three of them fell off the trailer in the process and injured themselves.

Luckily, an ambulance was two vehicles ahead in the parade, and the rescue squad volunteers sprang into action, treating the twisted ankles and skinned elbows right there on the street, where the whole crowd could admire them.

The picture on the front page the next week was the last time Magnum P.I. was in *The Wakefield Journal*. Two rescue workers in rubber gloves and surgical masks were scraping his remains into plastic bags. The Methodist minister, Roy Weinberger, stood in the background with his Bible open. He was actually praying for an injured hula dancer but, like Bug always said, nobody wants to know what's really going on.

The headline over the story and the picture was appropriately framed by Bug.

Magnum killed in fall from volcano
Local rescuers save lives of three others

PART TWO

SNAKES ALIVE

Winter months are slow around here. Being only marginally in the South, Wakefield has snow in January and sometimes even February. Black ice is a fact of life from late December through early March.

Though marginal we are, "South" is the truly operative word here. You'd think that after years of experiencing winter weather, we'd be used to it. You'd think wrong. Augusta County shuts down at the first hint of frost. Schools close, grocery stores sell out of bread and toilet paper, and residents settle in for the long hibernation necessary to survive blinding snow flurries and sub-forty-degree temperatures.

As a consequence of these bitter conditions, there is very little news to report at *The Wakefield Journal* between Thanksgiving and Easter. My days are mostly spent taking pictures of pitifully undernourished snowmen and car wrecks. I also get some good mileage out of the food pantry program sponsored by the Mennonites. They're one of the few groups in Augusta County still moving about outdoors in January. Most of the Mennonites here are a liberal sect from Canada, so when Augusta County natives are shivering under six quilts and turning up the space heaters as high as they go, the Mennonites are adding socks under their sandals and wearing long sleeves with their hiking shorts.

But come mid-March, when the world tilts back on its axis and stores switch their ice melt displays for flower seed, things start to pick back up again. The local folks trade in their insulated coveralls for sweaters and coats, and the Canadian Mennonites turn up the air conditioning and begin reporting to the hospital with heat stroke. Schools open, trees bud, flowers bloom, and snakes crawl.

I hate snakes.

I was reminded of this fact while working on a story about the increase in heat-related health emergencies among the Mennonites. Bug Wake, my publisher and editor, came out of his office as fast as a seventy-four-year-old man with two knee replacements could run.

"T.D., I got a hot one for you!" Bug said. Every story was a hot one for him, so I didn't get too excited.

"Oh, yeah? What is it?"

"A fellow over at Indian Springs was planting his beans and found a cobra," Bug said.

"You mean the car? Those things are rare."

Bug looked at me like I was stupid. "Not the car, the snake. You know, a cobra. Riki-Tiki-Tavi, spit poison in your eye, kill your babies. That kinda cobra."

I returned Bug's look. "Cobras live in India."

"Well, I told you it was Indian Springs."

Bug was beginning to get senile.

"I mean India in Asia. *The Jungle Book*, Mowgli, tigers?"

"I know where you're talking about. I'm old, not stupid. I'm telling you, Junior Brooks says he found a cobra in his bean patch. Get over there and take a picture."

Bug turned around abruptly, reaching for his cane, only to find it was still in his office. He limped slowly back inside then turned around to give one last instruction.

"See if he's got a goose you can put beside it. Nobody here knows what a mongoose is anyway."

Bug slammed his door and turned up the volume on the men's basketball tournament, leaving me to my snake hunt.

Indian Springs was twenty miles away over some of the worst roads in Augusta County. It would normally be a forty-minute drive, but since I was going to see a man about a snake, it took me an hour.

I really do hate snakes.

Junior Brooks' house was up a narrow dirt road lined with broken-down trailers. It wasn't really a farm, just an old farmhouse with peeling yellow paint and a dusty pickup out front. The garden stretched one hundred feet down the hill from the front yard to the edge of the road.

Junior himself was a behemoth of a man in baggy overalls and a Skoal baseball cap. He sat spraddle-legged on a cane-bottomed chair propped against the tailgate of his truck. A fish aquarium sat beside him, the top covered with a piece of plywood. Junior was using the plywood as a table for a plate of pickled eggs and a frosty Budweiser can.

I unfolded my legs from my ten-year-old Camaro and started toward him, displaying the camera prominently in front of me so Junior would know who I was.

"Good mornin'!" I called, eyeing the aquarium cautiously. "Are you Mr. Brooks?"

"I sure am. Are you the picture man?"

"That's me. I'm T.D. Duff." I stuck out my hand.

Junior squeezed until the bones cracked then drew back, leaving my hand aching and covered with pink vinegar and egg yolk.

"Good to meet ya," Junior said. "Want a pickled egg?"

"No, thanks, I just had some," I said, wiping my hand inconspicuously on the back of my pants leg. I made a mental note to stop at home and change my clothes before I went back to the office.

"Bug Wake says you found a…uh…snake," I said, looking in vain at the aquarium.

"I didn't just find any snake. I found a cobra."

"A cobra, huh? Not many of those around here."

"No, sir. I'm sixty-one and I ain't never seen one before. 'Cept on T.V., that is. I watch *Wild Kingdom* reruns all the time."

"Is that where you learned about cobras?"

"You got that right. I know all about 'em," Junior bragged.

"So you know where they live and everything, huh?" I asked pointedly.

"Yep. That's the one thing I couldn't figure out—how it got over here from India, but I figured some college kid had him for a pet and got tired of him. It's kinda like that tiger they killt down in Florida here while back. They're from India, too, but there it was, right in the middle of Orlando."

I couldn't argue with most of that logic, though I couldn't see some college kid keeping a cobra for a pet. Still, it made the glass aquarium look a lot less like a secure holding cell for a snake.

I backed up a few steps and switched to my telephoto lens before getting down on my hands and knees and peering through the glass. The aquarium was absolutely empty.

"Uh, Junior? Could the snake get out of that aquarium?"

Junior contemplated the aquarium. "I guess it probably could. Why?"

Not willing to take the chance that Junior might have just imagined the cobra, I chose my words carefully.

"I don't see him anywhere."

"Well, of course you don't," Junior said. "The sun's too hot to leave him out here in that glass cage. Why, I bet it don't even get that hot in the jungle."

"Oh," I said. "Where is he?"

"He's in the house," Junior replied, stuffing the rest of his egg into his mouth and brushing his hands together. "Come on and I'll show you."

Junior heaved his six-foot-four-inch, three-hundred-and-ninety-pound body out of his chair and waddled toward the front porch with me trailing behind.

Junior held the door for me then stepped inside. "Get you a chair, Pitcher Man. I'll get the cobra," he said.

"Where is it?" I asked, not so much curious as apprehensive.

"You know how them snake charmer fellers keep cobras in baskets? My wife's got a whole set of them things, so I picked it up on the hoe and put it in one of them."

Junior disappeared into the kitchen then reappeared two seconds later, white as a sheet.

"It's gone," he said.

"What's gone?" I asked, my eyes bugging out as I cast desperate glances under the tables.

"The cat turned over the basket and it's gone," he said.

Social conventions to the winds, my feet were already up on the couch.

"You mean the cat's gone?" I asked hopefully, picturing a contented and sleepy snake lying on the kitchen floor with a kitty-sized lump in its middle.

"No! The snake's gone," Junior said, joining me in standing on the couch.

"Maybe it went outside," I suggested.

"Maybe it came in here," Junior countered.

I judged the distance from the couch to the front door and made a leap for it. I was outside in less than a second and cleared the six steps down to the front yard without touching a single one. Junior was waiting for me when I got there.

"How did you...?" I asked.

"I may be big, but I'm quick on my feet," he panted.

"What are you gonna do? That thing's loose inside," I said.

"I'm gonna leave before Martha gets home," Junior replied.

"What's she gonna do?"

"She's gonna kill me," he said.

"No, I mean what's she gonna do about the snake?"

"The question is, what's the snake gonna do about her," Junior corrected. "If the poor thing bites her, it's done for."

"You've gotta get that snake out of there," I said. "You can't stay in the same house with it."

"I know that," Junior said. "Why do you think I'm out here?"

"Okay, let's calm down a minute," I said, taking deep breaths and encouraging Junior to do the same. "What can we do to get the snake out of the house?"

Junior took a few deep breaths then suddenly snapped his fingers. "I know. We'll burn it out," he said.

I gave him my best withering look.

"No! Wait...you're right. I can't do that," he said.

"How did you carry it in there?"

"I used a hoe, but it was outside then where I could see it. I ain't getting down on my hands and knees to look under the couch for it." He snapped his fingers. "I got it! Roger Shepherd."

"Who's Roger Shepherd?"

"Who's Roger Shepherd? You ain't from around here, are you?" Junior eyed me suspiciously.

"Yes, I am," I snapped, glaring back at him. "I grew up on Falls River. But I don't know any Roger Shepherd."

"Well, Roger Shepherd is only the most famousest snake hunter in Augusta County," Junior said. He hurried over to the chair, grabbed the cordless phone off the ground, and dialed a number.

"Roger? This is Junior...Junior Brooks... That's right. Well, listen. I got a snake for you," Junior said. "No. Better than a copperhead... Nope. Better than a rattler or a cottonmouth, too. It's a cobra... Never you mind where I got it. If you want it, you better get over here to my house and get it before I call Nosh Jones."

Junior pushed the button to hang up the phone and sat back down in his creaky old chair.

"He'll be here. Nosh Jones is tryin' to beat Roger out for the title of best snake hunter. If he was to get ahold of a cobra, he'd have it clinched."

Sure enough, Roger's Jeep CJ5 skidded into the driveway with a cloud of dust not five minutes later and Roger jumped out wearing knee-high camouflage boots and safety goggles.

"Where is it?" he asked. "You didn't call Nosh Jones, did you?"

"Now, Roger, you know I wouldn't do you that way," Junior told him, patting him reassuringly on the shoulder. "I was just pullin' your leg to get you to hurry."

"Well, I hurried. Where's the snake?"

"In the house," Junior said.

"Well, let's go get him."

"You go get him; you're the snake hunter," Junior replied.

"Okay. Where's he at?" Roger asked.

"In the house," Junior said.

"Where at in the house?" Roger pressed.

"Like I said, you're the snake hunter."

Roger, the most famousest snake hunter in Augusta County, paled visibly.

"You mean you got a cobra loose in the house?"

Junior nodded slowly and gave Roger a sympathetic grin.

Roger looked at me for confirmation. I nodded, too.

Roger looked at the house then back at the Jeep, as though contemplating whether he should risk his life or his reputation. Finally, he took a long pole with a hook on the end out of the Jeep, squared his shoulders, and started for the steps.

"I'm goin' in," he announced.

Roger was gone a long time. I could hear the sound of furniture moving and glass breaking inside the house, but Junior studiously ignored it. Once in a while he'd wince at a particularly loud crash, but he never said a word. After a half-hour, it grew quiet in the house. As the silence stretched to five minutes, sweat started to bead on Junior's forehead.

"Do you think he's all right?" I asked.

Junior looked worried. "He's the best snake hunter around."

I started to walk toward the house when the door flew open and Roger came out holding the pole in front of him, an eighteen-inch-long snake dangling on the end. I quickly retreated to the other side of the Jeep.

"I got him!" Roger yelled, coming toward us with the snake.

Junior, much braver now that Roger was there to control the snake, got up and examined it from ten feet away.

"That's him all right," Junior said, as though some other snake might have been hiding in his house.

"Get one of them bags out of my Jeep and hold it open while I put him in it," Roger said.

Junior looked at me. I looked at Junior.

"I ain't holdin' no bag open while you put him in it," Junior said. "Besides, this reporter feller here come to take a pitcher of my cobra. He can't do that if it's in a bag."

"He ain't your cobra; he's my cobra," Roger said.

"I found him," Junior snapped.

"Yeah, but you lost him and had to call me to find him again," Roger argued. "Besides, you told me I could have him."

"Well, I changed my mind," Junior said.

"All right, I'll put him back." Roger turned back toward the house.

"Wait! You can have him," Junior said quickly. "But at least let me have my pitcher took with him."

Roger agreed and turned toward me, smiling a dazzling smile. Junior put his arm around Roger and smiled, too, pointing at the snake.

When they were done, Junior took the plywood off the top of the aquarium and Roger dropped the snake inside. Once the snake was safely behind glass and covered with plywood, I stepped from behind the Jeep to get a closer look.

"That doesn't look like a cobra," I said.

"Sure it does. Look at its hood," Roger said.

"Look at its color. It's orange."

"How do you know a cobra ain't orange?" Roger asked.

He had me there. I looked at the snake again. I couldn't believe it was really a cobra.

"What are you going to do with it?" I asked, changing the subject.

"I'm gonna sell it," Roger said.

"Who would buy it? A zoo?"

"Of course not," he scoffed. "I'll sell it to a church."

"A church!?"

"Yeah, a church. That's where I sell all the snakes I catch," he confided.

"You mean there are still snake-handling churches in Augusta County?" I asked, shocked at the prospect.

"There's a few," Roger said. "But don't put that in the paper. They like to keep a low profile."

He gathered up the aquarium and drove away. Junior picked up his hoe and his bag of seed beans and started back for the garden.

"Thanks for comin' out, Pitcher Man," he said. "Do me a favor and don't say nothin' about that snake bein' in the house. Martha'll kill me."

"How are you gonna explain the broken glass?"

Junior stopped and thought a minute. "I don't know. She won't be home for another two hours, though. I'll think of something."

I spent the next day looking at snake pictures in library books while I waited for a call back from Fred Gatling, a herpetologist from the Atlanta Zoo. When he finally called back, I told him about Junior Brooks' unwelcome visitor.

"Anyway, he says he found a cobra," I finished.

When Gatling finally stopped laughing, he informed me that what Junior found and what Roger caught was (surprise) definitely not a cobra.

"What you and your friends have there is a hognose snake," Gatling said. "You may have heard of it before but not by that name. Most people in those parts call them blowing vipers. Cobras don't even live in this country."

"I know cobras don't live in this country. I just didn't know what it was," I said. "I've never seen a blowing viper."

"They really put on a show, don't they?" Gatling giggled. "Surely the snake catcher knew what it was, though. I think that ol' boy was just blowing smoke up your skirt."

"So it's not some exotic snake that somebody turned loose?" I asked.

Gatling laughed again.

"No! They're all over the South. Blowing vipers are legendary. They puff up and hiss and act mean, but if you don't leave them alone, they roll over and play dead."

"You mean they don't bite?" I asked.

"Not likely," Gatling said.

"They're not even poisonous?"

"Well, yeah, but their teeth are so far back in their mouths that they couldn't touch you with them even if they tried," Gatling said, stifling another laugh. "They use them to paralyze mice as they swallow them. Of course, that doesn't necessarily mean you shouldn't worry. I mean, what are you—a man or a mouse?"

Now I not only hated snakes in general, I hated this particular snake for making a fool out of me. I also hated Fred Gatling. And Roger Shepherd, the most famous snake hunter in Augusta County, ranked right down there with the snake and Gatling on my list of people and things to hate. I hung up the phone and called Roger.

"Roger!" I said. "T.D. Duff here. You know, *The Wakefield Journal*? I found out what that snake was."

"It was a cobra," Roger said shortly.

"No, cobras don't live in the United States," I informed him.

"This one does," Roger answered.

"Well, yeah, but it's not a cobra. It's a blowing viper."

There was silence at the other end of the line.

"Hello? Roger?"

"You didn't tell nobody else, did you?" Roger asked.

"Well, not yet. But you know that picture's gonna be in the newspaper this week."

"No, it ain't!" Roger yelled into the phone. "I didn't tell you that you could put my picture in the paper."

"Sure you did...you posed for it and everything," I reminded him.

"I didn't know where you was from," he said. "You can't put that picture in the paper and say it's a blowin' viper. You'll ruin my reputation."

"But, Roger, it is a blowing viper."

"Says you," he said.

"No, says Fred Gatling at the Atlanta Zoo."

"He ain't never seen it," Roger protested.

"Roger, did you sell that snake?" I asked, suddenly suspicious.

There was another long silence.

"Roger?"

"You can't do this to me!"

"Do what?"

"You think a snake-handling preacher wouldn't know a blowing viper when he sees it? You put my picture in the paper and say I caught a blowing viper and everybody will laugh at me. You put my picture in the paper say I caught a cobra and everybody will laugh at me. I'm ruined. I'll never sell another snake in this county. You can't put my picture in the paper!"

"If a snake-handling preacher would know what it is, then you should, too," I said, feeling righteously indignant. "You knew, but you tried to make me and Junior Brooks believe it was really a cobra."

"I wanna talk to your boss!" Roger raved.

"Fine," I said. Bug would tell him. There was no way Bug would pass up a chance to put a cobra or a blowing viper in the paper. It was just too good an opportunity to pass up. Roger Shepherd would soon find out what we would and would not put the paper. I yelled for Bug to pick up the other phone.

"T.D., we're not gonna use that picture of the snake in the paper," Bug said five minutes later after he hung up the phone and came out of his office.

"What!? I've spent two days working on that. You sent me out there. You even told me to find a goose to pose with it."

"Well, you didn't find a goose. Besides, a man's reputation is at stake here. Sorry," Bug said, hobbling back to his office on his cane.

So there it was. I had been betrayed by the one man I could count on to do the cheesy thing. He did something even cheesier than I could imagine.

But it made Roger Shepherd happy. I heard his name whispered in grocery stores. The story was spreading like wildfire, even without the newspaper. The most famousest snake hunter in Augusta County had caught a beaut—a real live king cobra, eight feet long and spitting venom.

He had clinched his place in Augusta County's snake-hunting pecking order. Nosh Jones was sunk.

Unfortunately, Nosh Jones didn't give up that easily.

Roger Shepherd's exploits with the "cobra" had been traveling the gossip circuit for three weeks when a greasy-haired man in a white t-shirt, dirty blue jeans, and knee-high boots came into the office. I'd seen boots like those before.

"Are you the Pitcher Man?" he asked.

I knew immediately that this was my big chance, and I'd better take it.

"Sorry," I said, stepping around the man and going out the door. "He's gone to lunch."

I was halfway down the sidewalk, heading for the parking lot, when the man caught up with me, boots and all.

"You know, I was in the union for twenty years," he said, trotting along beside me. "When lunchtime come, there couldn't nothin' hold me on the job."

"That's the way to be." I picked up my pace a little more.

"No, sir. I can't fault a man for takin' his break on time," he continued, not taking the hint. "You mind if I go with you?"

I tried to think of a polite way to say I did mind, but I couldn't, so I just nodded and changed directions, making for the corner drugstore instead of my car.

"I'm Nosh Jones," the man said, sticking out his hand. Two fingers were missing.

I shook his hand politely as I hurried down the street. "T.D. Duff."

"You bein' a reporter feller and everything, I guess you heard about Roger Shepherd catchin' a cobra," Nosh said.

"Cobras don't live around here," I mumbled noncommittally.

"That's right, they don't," Nosh grinned. "And if they don't live around here, he couldn't have caught one, now could he?"

"Guess not," I confirmed.

"And since it ain't never been in the newspaper, he ain't got no proof he ever caught one either, has he?"

"Not that I know of," I answered.

Nosh Jones had followed me into McNeeley's Drug Store and plopped down onto a stool beside me at the lunch counter.

"Gimme the soup-bean dinner," Nosh told the waitress.

"Special. To go," I added quickly.

"Make mine to go, too," Nosh yelled after her. "I'm glad you got your'n to go. I got something in the truck I want to show you."

Great, I thought, *another cobra story*. But as it turns out, Nosh Jones was a little more realistic than Roger Shepherd.

"I was cuttin' weeds this morning, and I killed three copperheads..."

"Wait a second," I interrupted him. "You mean you kill snakes? I thought you caught snakes."

"I do," Nosh said. "But all my cages are full right now. Since that cobra story started goin' around, my business has dried up. Everybody's goin' to that durned Roger Shepherd for their snakes. Anyhow, I done killed three <u>purty</u> copperheads when I came upon the biggest one I've ever seen in my whole life."

"Really?" I asked, trying to imagine why anybody would be so excited about such a find.

"Really. And I got to thinkin'. If I could get a pitcher in the paper with that big ol' copperhead, I'd be a notch up on Roger Shepherd. He just <u>says</u> he caught a cobra. But I'll be able to <u>prove</u> I found the biggest copperhead ever seen in Augusta County."

I nodded and looked at him.

"Well, how about it?" he asked.

"How about what?"

"Will you take our pitcher?"

"Whose picture?" I asked.

"Me and the copperhead," Nosh said.

"Oh! Yeah, sure. Where is it?"

"In the back of my truck. I'm parked right over by your office."

Our food came and I walked back down the street with Nosh. I hate snakes, but how bad could it be to take a picture of a dead one? After all, it wasn't like it could bite me or anything.

When we got back to the office, I set my food inside on the counter and went to get my camera while Nosh began undoing the assortment of rubber straps that held the tailgate up on his truck.

When I got back, Nosh had pulled a Coleman cooler from the back of the truck and was opening it up. Inside, on a bed of ice, lay the biggest copperhead I had ever seen. It was as thick as a man's wrist and must have been four feet long. Nosh grabbed it by the neck and the tail and stretched it out full length. It was impressive.

I snapped a couple of pictures while Nosh smiled and held the snake. Passersby gawked. A crowd gathered. Not one to miss a detail, I asked Nosh just how long the snake was.

"You know what? I ain't even measured him yet," Nosh said. "Here, hold him 'til I get a ruler out of the truck."

Nosh thrust the cold, dead snake into my hands before I could say no. It was then that I realized that the cold dead snake was really a cold live snake and the warmth of the April sun reflecting off the asphalt was rapidly turning it into a <u>warm</u> live snake. Warm snakes don't like to be held.

Now, I have never thought of myself as a coward. I have never hidden my eyes at scary movies or puked at the sight of blood. I've never slept with the light on, or closed the closet door to keep the monsters in. But I hate snakes.

When I came to, I was lying in the hospital with a cold compress on the back of my head and the smell of ammonia lingering in my nostrils. My left hand was swaddled in bandages.

I groaned and a squat, fifty-something nurse with bleached blond hair walked around the head of the examining table and into my field of view.

"Well, well. You're awake. You certainly did give us a scare," she said. "I'm Martha, your nurse. I'm so glad to finally meet you. My husband, Junior, thinks the world of you after you helped Roger Shepherd catch that cobra snake that crawled into our house."

"What happened?" I asked.

"You mean before you fainted or after?"

"Uh, after."

"Well," she began, "as soon as you fainted and let go of that snake's tail and it started wiggling, the crowd scattered."

At least God had some mercy.

"Is that when it bit me?" I asked, holding up my bandaged hand.

"Oh, it didn't bite you! Goodness, no."

"It didn't?"

"No! Nosh Jones did."

"Nosh Jones bit me?"

"Well, you can't blame the man. It was the only way he could get your fingers from around the snake's neck. You were strangling the poor thing. A snake like that is worth a lot of money."

"Nosh Jones bit me?"

"Now, honey, we did a blood test and he doesn't have any diseases or anything. Besides, he saved you from the snake."

"How do you figure?"

"As soon as you let go of it, he snatched it off your face and threw it back in the cooler. Why, a bite from a copperhead that big would have hurt something fierce."

My hand throbbed. I could feel the imprint of all six of Nosh Jones' teeth.

"When can I go home?" I asked.

"Oh, any time now. As soon as you get your tetanus shot. Now, undo your pants and roll over."

The needle entered my right buttock at the exact same moment that Bug limped through the door and snapped the picture.

It was on the front page the next week, right next to the one of Nosh Jones triumphantly holding the four-foot copperhead. It was almost worth the embarrassment just because of the impact it would have on Roger Shepherd's business.

After all, Shepherd only said he caught a cobra. Nosh Jones had proof of his copperhead, and it was right there in black and white. The headline was a Bug Wake special:

Journal reporter survives attack by giant snake
Jones, famous local snake hunter, nabs rogue reptile

PART THREE

THE LAST WAKE

Reporters see a lot of death. We see it at car wrecks, hunting accidents, domestic disputes, and the occasional after-game nightclub incident. We probably see as much death as paramedics; we just see it from a greater distance.

Listen in on a reporter, a cop, and a funeral director talk about death, and you'd never guess it is so serious.

As much as reporters love to joke about death, Bug Wake was downright ecstatic when someone passed away. He wasn't happy the person was gone, but he was tickled to death that he would get to plan a wake. Maybe it was the fact that the celebrations came to be known as Wake's Wakes or maybe it was the fact that he was the last surviving descendent of Wakefield's founder and namesake, Patrick Wake, and he felt a certain civic obligation to see long-time residents off to the great beyond.

I never really figured it out; I just accepted it as a fact of life and death in Augusta County.

Growing up here, I had heard of Wake's Wakes ever since I was a kid. They were mostly reserved for Wakefield residents, but occasionally someone who had been born in the town and moved away was honored with the events as well. After I went to work at Bug's paper, *The Wakefield Journal*, he always insisted that I attend.

"T.D., everybody deserves a good wake and everybody deserves to have the most prominent people in the community pay their last respects," Bug said. "You working for me and your name being in *The Journal* every week makes you prominent, whether you like it or not."

So Bug would drag me down the street to the Augusta Funeral Home chapel, to a local church, or sometimes down to the VFW and start in on an all-night binge of eating or drinking or both, depending on the religious persuasion of the dearly departed's family.

It was at least a twice-a-month event in Wakefield, and Bug always looked forward to them. He scanned the obituaries that the two funeral homes sent over every morning before Anabelle could even set them in type, and then he'd pick out the people he knew well and start calling their families and making arrangements. He even made me write my own obituary and he put it in a special file in his office.

"Every reporter should write his own obituary," Bug lectured. "You don't want some hack to do it for you, do you?"

Considering that Bug was the only hack I knew, I quickly complied and turned in the finished obit by the end of the day. It wasn't the most pleasant task I've ever undertaken, but it did make me think about my life and what I was doing with it.

It was July when Bug first broached the subject of his own death to me. Will Tyler, who was seventy-eight years old and a classmate of Bug's, got kicked in the head while shoeing his racking horse and thus became the guest of honor at one of Wake's Wakes. We were sitting in the VFW lifting our glasses and toasting old Will's World War II service, his fine horses, his champion fighting cocks, his beagles, and just about everything else anybody could think of to toast, when Bug hobbled up on his quad-cane and sat down in the booth beside me.

"Now this, T.D., is a wake to be remembered," Bug said, looking out proudly over the assembled crowd of veterans and "B members," who joined the VFW so they could buy bootleg beer.

"Some of us may remember it, but I wouldn't count on it," I said, taking another sip of my beer.

"No, I mean I want you to remember this wake," Bug said. "I want one just like it for myself."

I hadn't expected that. Bug never seemed depressed at his wakes and never talked about his own death. I just assumed the old man would be there forever. I stole a quick glance at him and saw something I'd never seen before. Bug Wake, who was often grouchy, often excited, and always self-assured, was sad.

His white mustache seemed to droop even more than usual, and his hound-dog eyes were rimmed with red.

"Aw, Bug, you'll be holding a wake for me before anybody has one for you."

Bug shook his head. "No. You're young. What are you now—twenty-six? Twenty-seven? I'm seventy-eight. There aren't any more Wakes left around here. I'm the last of the line. But I've tried to teach you everything I know. You're the one who'll have to see me off."

With that, Bug struggled to his feet and went back to join his old friends. My heart wasn't in it after that. For all his faults, all his butchering of the news, and all my griping about it, I had grown close to Bug Wake. I finished my beer and left quietly, walking the two blocks back to my apartment over the old theater.

The next morning, I had to use my key to get into the office for the first time since I began working at *The Journal* five years before. Bug was always there before me, but that morning, he was nowhere in sight. I was a little apprehensive after his talk of dying the night before, and as the day wore on, I became positively worried. Anabelle came in and went to pick up the mail at the post office, and Bug still hadn't shown up. Milton Lee, an embalmer at the Augusta Funeral Home, delivered the latest obituary, but Bug still wasn't there. I called his home and got no answer. I had made up my mind to go over to the old Victorian house where he lived and peek through the windows when Bug finally walked through the door.

"Bug? Is everything all right?" I asked, careful not to say anything about his health.

"Of course it is. Why wouldn't it be?" he questioned grumpily.

"Oh, no reason. I'm just used to you being here before me."

Bug harrumphed and limped into his office, shoving the door open with his cane since his free arm was filled with envelopes and papers. He slammed the door behind him and sat down at his desk, ignoring the ratty brown recliner that he normally used.

I went back to work, casting furtive glances through the glass door of Bug's office and wondering what was up. The television, which was perpetually set to ESPN or CNN, never came on, and one line of the telephone was busy all day as Bug made call after call.

When I left at five, Bug was still sitting at his desk, talking on the phone and making notes on the bundle of papers in front of him. When I got to the office the next morning, he was already at his desk following the same routine as he had the day before. If he hadn't changed shirts, I would have thought he had been there all night.

I resigned myself to the new Bug and got busy on the school board story from the night before. I was sure Bug would come out of his funk sooner or later.

I was just putting the finishing touches on the story when Bug's door finally flew open and he came out, apparently back to normal.

"T.D., I got a hot one for you," he said.

Ordinarily those words sent a chill down my back and sent me scrambling for an excuse about how I was already working on a different story, but this time I was actually relieved to hear them.

"Hey, great! I just finished one up. What is it?"

"You're gonna write my life story," Bug said.

"Your life story?"

"Yeah, sort of," Bug hedged.

"What do you mean sort of?" I asked, my mind suddenly groping for an excuse after all.

"It's actually my obituary. You're gonna write it," Bug said.

"But you always said every reporter should write his own obituary. You mean you never did?"

"Of course not. That's morbid. I only told you that to give you something to do. You looked bored."

At Bug's insistence, I dropped everything and followed him into his office with my notebook and recorder. Bug took the recliner, I sat in the desk chair, and we began the long process of reviewing his life. He started with the mundane—born in Wakefield, married twice, divorced once, widowed once, no children—and quickly moved to the unbelievable—his meeting as a high school student with Franklin Roosevelt during the 1932 campaign, his service as an OSS agent during World War II, and his advice to Harry Truman that he drop the big one on Japan.

"Then there was the time me and Bob Hope were doing this big USO show in the South Pacific..."

"Wait a minute. You expect people to believe you knew Bob Hope?" I asked, unable to contain myself any longer.

"Not 'knew'...know," Bug insisted. "I still get a Christmas card from him and Doris every year."

"Bug..."

He struggled to his feet, pulled a scrapbook the size of a tabloid newspaper and three inches thick off a bookshelf, thumbed through a few pages, and then laid it on the desk. Sure enough, there was a photo of Bob Hope and a much younger, though perfectly recognizable, Bug Wake dancing together on a stage, surrounded by beautiful young women in sarongs.

"Okay, so you danced with Bob Hope. But didn't he always pull soldiers out of the crowd and put them on stage?" I questioned stubbornly.

"Turn the page," Bug urged.

The next page and the next, and the next, held Christmas cards from Hope, some referring to Bug's help with his shows. I just shook my head in wonder. Bug was a real-life Forrest Gump. As I continued to turn pages, I encountered photos of Bug with celebrities great and small. There was a picture of him interviewing John F. Kennedy. Another showed him at a radio microphone with Ernest Tubb and Little Jimmy Dickens. In between were pictures of Bug at mundane events like school board meetings, ribbon cuttings, and the first run of *The Journal* on its then-new offset press.

"What's with the radio picture with Ernest Tubb?" I asked.

"I used to own the station here," Bug explained. "Ernest and Jimmy came down to help open it up."

"So what happened to the station?" I asked, looking at the unfamiliar WKFD call letters on the microphone.

"I shut it down when Glen Campbell got his first number-one song," Bug said.

And so it went for days on end. Bug sat in his recliner and poured out anecdote after anecdote about his life. After a week, during which we had to use Associated Press stories on the front-page of the paper because I was too busy with Bug to write anything, we finally completed the interviews. I put the finishing touches on the obituary just before lunch, three days after I finished interviewing him. While Bug wasn't looking, I called longtime residents to ask their opinions of him and stuck some of the better insults into the story.

"Well, Bug, I know you're dying to read it, so here it is," I said, handing him the opus.

"No bad jokes, please," Bug said. "I'll let you know what I want changed."

Bug spent the rest of the day reading his own obituary while I sat nervously at my desk and watched him through the glass door. Occasionally, I'd see the old man chuckle and a couple of times he laughed out loud. At 4:55 p.m., just as I was getting ready to leave for the day, Bug brought the story back and laid it on my desk without a word. Except for a few corrected typos, he hadn't changed anything.

The next Monday, Bug was absent again. There was a note on my desk explaining that he had a doctor's appointment and didn't expect to be in. In fact, he expected to be admitted to the hospital and requested the honor of my presence there at noon.

I rushed up to the hospital a half-hour early and found Bug lying in a bed with an I.V. in his arm.

"Bug, what happened?" I questioned, shocked by the change.

"I got old," he said. "I didn't think anybody would notice."

I couldn't help but laugh, but the old man never cracked a smile.

"I didn't want to tell anybody," Bug said. "T.D., I've got pancreatic cancer. The doctors found it a month ago, but they said it's pretty far advanced, and it moves fast. I suspected it, but I was too old to let them operate so I didn't tell the doctors anything was bothering me. I finally had to tell them so they could give me something for the pain. Now my kidneys are trying to shut down. T.D., if they quit functioning, I'm not gonna last long."

"Now, Bug, they can do dialysis. A lot of people live a long life, even with these kinds of problems," I said, trying to soothe myself as much as him.

"I've already lived a long life, T.D. I don't want to spend the rest of it hooked up to some machine. If it comes down to that, I want to just go on out. And the doctor already knows it. I signed a living will as soon as I found out."

So there it was. Bug Wake, the man who had sent so many of his friends off with parties and a toast to their afterlife, was dying himself. I didn't know what to say, and I wouldn't have trusted myself to speak if I <u>had</u> known. My lungs felt as though they had lost all capacity for air, and my throat was so tight that I wasn't sure I could have made a sound.

Bug saw the dampness in my eyes and looked quickly away at the papers on his tray table.

"T.D., I'm the last Wake there is. I don't have any children. My brothers and sisters are all dead. I want you to promise me something."

"Sure, Bug, anything."

"I want you to make sure *The Journal* doesn't fold up. It's been in my family since 1893. I don't want it to die with me," Bug said, his eyes tearing up, too.

I swallowed hard and nodded. "I'll do my best, Bug, but I don't know what to do with it. You'll have to tell me who gets it. You've got some nephews and nieces, but you didn't tell me their names when I did the obit."

"You don't need to know," Bug said. "*The Journal* is going to you. You've worked for me five years now. That's longer than anybody ever put up with me there. You're closer than any of my kin, and I trust you. I know you haven't always liked the way I ran the paper, and that's why I trust you. You'll do what you think is right." And that's how I became a newspaper entrepreneur. I didn't buy it or plan it; it was foisted upon me by a lonely old man.

I sat with Bug for an hour at lunch and after work every day for the next two weeks as he declined quickly from his old, vigorous self to a shell. He couldn't eat. The nurses said he rarely slept. But when the next two editions of *The Journal* came out, he read them front to back and placed his stamp of approval on each one.

"You'll do well," Bug said, handing the newspaper back to me. "When I die, there's a list of people in my middle desk drawer that I want you to notify. The phone numbers are all there. Most of them probably won't come to the funeral, but I want them to know. And don't forget my wake."

Bug lapsed into a coma that night. He died four days later—literally drowned in his own fluids. The list of friends he left included Bob Hope, the Kennedy family, and several country music stars. Bug was right. Most of them didn't come to the funeral, but all of them sent flowers and cards. The wake, held at the VFW, lasted two days and Bug's friends proclaimed it one of the best Augusta County had ever seen—a wake entirely fitting for a man who loved them so well. I added a couple paragraphs about it to the top of Bug's obituary, right under the funeral information, and ran it on the front page of *The Journal*.

It was midnight when I put the paper to bed, after typing Bug's final headline:

The last Wake in Wakefield
Media mogul Jasper "Bug" Wake succumbs after an amazing life

PART FOUR

KYLE PELPHRY
AND THE KILLER POSSUM

Being that the Appalachian Mountains are the last great wilderness area of the eastern United States, it stands to reason that they have their share of wild animals. It also stands to reason that those animals just can't resist wandering down out of the hills sometimes to see what we humans are up to. And our local hunters here in Augusta County very often wander up into the hills to see what the animals are up to.

And shoot them.

The Wakefield Journal runs a dozen photos of dead deer every year, the proud hunter standing nearby with his bow or his rifle. It's a tradition Bug Wake started, and I didn't have the heart to end it after he passed on and left the paper to me.

Tony Fitzhugh got his trophy in mid-November and proudly laid a three-by-five picture, still wet from the one-hour-photo place, on the front counter at the newspaper office. There it was: tongue hanging out, blood running down the fender. But it wasn't a deer.

"What the heck is this?" I asked.

"It's a deer," Tony said, squinting at the picture.

"Are you sure?"

"Of course I'm sure," he said.

"Uh, Tony, I'm no expert, but doesn't a deer have antlers?"

"The bucks do, but this is a doe. The state let us hunt 'em this year."

"Tony, a doe is a female deer, isn't it?" I asked, turning the picture to the light.

Tony squinted at the photo again.

"Sure it is. Why?"

"What time of day did you shoot him...er...her?"

"Well, it musta been about noon, 'cause I was gettin' awful hungry," he said. "You see, I was on my way to the tree stand yesterday morning before daylight, and as I was crossin' the creek, I slipped and fell. Well, when I did, I dropped all my food, my extra ammo—I even lost my glasses."

I suddenly felt enlightened.

"Anyway, I lost all my food and I was thinkin' to myself that I'd have to waste half a day of huntin' so I could go home and eat. I was startin' to get real hungry when this big ol' doe here wandered out of a cornfield and right under my tree stand. Well, sir, I got her. Just like they say: 'one shot, one kill.'"

"Ah. Are you sure you want to put it in the paper?" I asked delicately.

"Hell, yeah, I want to put it in the paper! Do you know how much I ended up payin' for this deer? I bought a license, a deer tag, my food, my ammo. New glasses alone are gonna cost me four hundred dollars. If I figured it all up, it'd probably be twenty bucks a pound."

"I'd say it's gonna cost you a lot all right," I agreed. "But are you sure the satisfaction of killing it isn't enough?"

"I'm sure. Look, I can't have the head mounted because it ain't got antlers, but I can have my picture put in the paper. Besides, if you'll put it in for me, I'll bring you a nice juicy steak off it."

I declined quickly. "No need. I'll put it in for you, but only if you insist."

He insisted. I put it in.

Kyle Pelphry, the local game warden, was not amused. Neither was Richard Welton, the farmer whose mule had wandered into Tony's sights.

Tony didn't think it was very funny either, especially after he picked up his new glasses and got a good look at his doe. He swore the meat wasn't half bad, though.

That was just the first of several wild game fiascos that winter and spring. Come May, Kyle was about worn out from chasing through the woods.

"I swear, T.D., if I didn't have a break between turkey season and Memorial Day weekend, I think I'd go plumb crazy," he said as we sat at the lunch counter at McNeeley's Drug Store. "I've heard every excuse twice and some of them three times."

"Every one?" I asked.

"Well, almost. Tony Fitzhugh's excuse is gonna stand a long time before anybody else uses it. Shooting a mule because you're too blind to tell it ain't a deer ain't much of an excuse."

Kyle had taken one bite of his reuben when his pager went off. He pushed the button a couple of times to read the message then threw a five on the counter and grabbed his sandwich.

"You might be interested in this. Somebody reported a bear at the housing project," Kyle said, heading for the door.

I asked for a box for my meal then followed along a few minutes behind Kyle. When I got to the apartment complex on the outskirts of Wakefield, Kyle was standing at the doorway of an apartment talking to a frantic-looking elderly woman in a housecoat.

"Of course I'm sure it was a bear! I've been leaving peanuts out for it every night. Well, I forgot them last night, and it tore into the garbage cans. I set them back up and it came back again. It's out there right now!"

"Right now?" Kyle asked as he craned his neck to see past the woman and through the back windows of her apartment.

"You can't see it from here. You'll have to go through the back door. Come in, hurry."

She dragged Kyle through the front and I uncapped my camera lens and went around the side of the house at what I felt was a safe distance from any bear that might be rummaging around in the backyard. I couldn't see anything, but there were several large trash cans behind the apartment. Two were turned over and another was shaking vigorously. Kyle peeped out the back door then came outside and looked over the top of the cans as I stood back a few feet and took pictures. A few seconds later, he relaxed and reached behind the cans. He came out with a large possum, holding it out at arm's length by the tail as it feigned death.

"Well, I got your bear right here," Kyle said. "It's just a hungry possum."

The woman, more flustered than ever now, looked at the possum, and then looked at Kyle and me.

"Well, I know there was a bear here," she said. "He's been here every night. I put out peanuts for him and he comes back and gets them."

"Have you ever actually seen him?" Kyle asked.

"Well, no. I go to bed at eight-thirty. But I know it's a bear. I hear him," she said.

"Well, Mrs. Lewis, I think you can stop worrying about a bear. But you shouldn't put out any more peanuts. It's against the law. When you feed bears, they lose their fear of humans. They're friendly as can be as long as you've got peanuts, but they get right upset when you run out."

"Oh, my! I hadn't thought of that," Mrs. Lewis said. "I'd better go to the store and get some more."

Kyle started to explain, but changed his mind and shut his mouth.

"Goodbye, Mrs. Lewis," he said. "You take care now."

I followed Kyle to the truck, where he placed the possum in a cage and slammed the tailgate.

"You get a good picture of that bear, T.D.?"

"Yeah, buddy," I confirmed.

"Good. Maybe that'll keep Mrs. Lewis from calling me out on false alarms anymore. Oh, and don't forget: we're playin' poker tonight at Larry's."

Kyle climbed in his truck and drove away with a wave. I talked briefly with Mrs. Lewis and decided to run the photo without mentioning that she had mistaken it for a bear. After all, there was no reason to embarrass the poor woman any more than she had already been embarrassed.

When I got back to the office, Anabelle was waiting to pounce.

"Where have you been? I've called everywhere to try and find you. Did you know there was a bear at the housing project?"

"No! Really?" I asked.

"Really. It was a great big one, too. Why, it was right there in Audrey Lewis' garbage cans."

"In the garbage cans, huh? Did they catch it?"

Anabelle shrugged and picked up her glasses, which were hanging on a chain down the front of her flowered dress, and began polishing them with a tissue.

"I don't know. You might still be able to get a picture of it if you hurry," she said.

I grinned and held up the camera. "I'm just teasing you, Anabelle. I've already been and I'll show you the pictures just as soon as I get them developed."

"Was it big and scary?" Anabelle asked breathlessly.

"It was huge, but I wasn't scared."

"You liar. I bet you were scared out of your pants."

"Don't say such things, Anabelle, I'll think you're flirting," I told her, heading back toward the darkroom.

"Oh, hush. I'm old enough to be your...older sister."

Actually, she was old enough to be my mother's sister, but I didn't want to say anything.

"You know what they say about older women, Anabelle."

When I developed the possum pictures, I dropped the black-and-white prints on Anabelle's desk in an envelope and rushed for the door. I heard her laughing all the way out in the parking lot as I left for the poker game.

Poker at Larry Stone's house is a tradition. Larry is an X-ray technician at the Augusta County Methodist Hospital. He and his wife, Hilda, a teacher, have a nice two-story brick house that sits high up on the hill in the west end of Wakefield, not far from the housing project.

Every Friday night, Hilda takes the kids to visit their grandparents and Larry invites Kyle, Danny Vaughn, and me over to play quarter-ante poker. That particular night just wasn't Kyle's night.

First he lost to me while holding two pair. Then he lost to Larry with three jacks. Finally, to add insult to injury, he folded a pair of queens only to have Danny win with a pair of threes.

"Damnation!" Kyle griped, throwing his cards back in the middle of the table. "I can't win for losin'."

"You ought to at least feel good for your friends," I said, dealing another hand. "We're makin' money. Ante up."

"You're makin' my money," he said.

"Wah! Wah!" Larry laughed, opening his fifth beer and drinking it straight down. He belched loudly and crushed the can. "You big baby."

"When you go home, you can cuddle up to your new pet. That'll make you feel better," Danny said soothingly.

"What new pet?"

"The possum."

"Oh, I turned him loose. He's probably all the way to Mrs. Lewis' house by now, if he made it across the highway."

"Where did you turn him loose?" I asked.

"I just told you: across the highway."

"You know you're just gonna have to go back there again, don't you?" Danny asked.

"Danny, it's a possum. What are the chances that he's gonna make it across the road?"

"The chicken did," Larry jibed, downing another beer.

"Only to show the possum that it was possible," Danny laughed.

"For a chicken maybe, but not for a possum," Kyle said. "Are we playin' jacks or better?"

"Guts," I said. "You got enough to bet?"

"Yeah, I'll bet a quarter."

Larry called and Danny raised another quarter. Larry and I called, but Kyle just looked at him.

"You got another pair of threes over there, I know by lookin' at you. I'll call and raise you."

Before Danny could toss in his coins, Kyle's pager went off. He ignored it until Danny called.

"Cards?" I asked.

Kyle's pager went off again.

"Are you gonna answer that thing or not?" Larry asked, his tongue as thick as a two-by-four.

Kyle threw two cards into the middle of the table and pulled his pager off his belt.

"I'll be damned. Mrs. Lewis' possum is back."

"I told you," Danny said, standing pat with the cards he had.

"You're bluffin'," Kyle replied, taking his cards. "I'll pay another quarter to see what you've got."

"What are you gonna do?" I asked, putting in my quarters.

"Yeah, Kyle, you can't let that poor old biddy sit out there with a possum problem," Larry said.

Kyle wiped Larry's spit out of his eye and studied his cards. "How many cards did you take?" he asked, focused on Larry.

"You're not supposed to be sleepin' at the table, partner," Larry said.

"He wasn't sleepin'; he was playin' possum," Danny said.

"We'll play this hand out and we'll all play possum," Kyle answered, matching Larry's bet. "I'll take a whole possum posse over to Mrs. Lewis'."

When the raises stopped, Danny laid down his hand to show three aces and I threw my pitiful pair of queens in. Kyle chuckled and laid down a full house, jacks over threes. He smirked triumphantly at Larry, who grinned like a possum and laid down a full house of his own.

"Cowboys and ei...eights," he burped.

Kyle groaned. "I'm goin' possum huntin'. Anybody comin' with me?"

"Yeah, I'll go," I said, gathering my jacket and my unused quarters.

"I wouldn't miss it for the world," Danny said. "How about you, Lar?"

"Hell, yeah, I'm goin'. Surely that woman didn't call in just to have you catch that same ol' possum again."

"No, dispatch says she reported a bear again," Kyle said, reading his pager and reaching for the telephone. "I'll call to let 'em know I'm goin', and I'll be ready."

When he hung up, we piled into Kyle's car and headed off to the housing project with flashlights. Larry, who had drunk quite a bit more than the rest of us since he didn't have to drive anywhere that night, brought along his cooler and the lasso he'd bought his son when they went to the rodeo.

The lights were off in Audrey Lewis' apartment when we pulled up, but she was watching out the side of the curtains and she opened the door a crack as soon as she saw Kyle.

"Hurry! He's around back," she whispered, her eyes the size of saucers.

Kyle nodded. "Don't worry, ma'am, we'll get him."

"Let's round him up, partners," Larry said, twirling the lasso. Kyle glared at him and started around the side of the house.

"Wait, have you got a cage with you?" I asked.

"No, they're all in my garage or in the back of my state truck," Kyle said. Since he was off duty, he was driving his Mustang.

"What are you gonna do with him when you catch him?" I asked.

"We're gonna corral that critter," Larry interrupted. Kyle ignored him.

"I'll throw him in the trunk of the car and deal with him when I get home."

"Don't you worry none, sonny, I'll lasso him and hog tie him, and you can put him right up in the front seat of the...buckboard with you," Larry said, hiccoughing before he could finish the sentence.

By this time we were all bunched together around Kyle, who was in an inordinate hurry to catch the possum and leave. We rounded the corner of the house at a fast walk and ran smack into the backend of the "possum." Unfortunately, this possum looked plime blank like a black bear.

Now, biologists will tell you that black bears are docile creatures that would rather run from a human than confront one. Most biologists have never rear-ended a black bear in the middle of the night.

The bear glared over its shoulder and growled a low, threatening growl. The growl was barely audible from ten feet away, but people on Falls River, five miles away, swear they heard us scream.

Kyle, Danny, and I nearly fell over each other as we scrambled backward to put some distance between us and the bear. Larry stood swaying in the wind and looking the bear dead in the eyes—all four of them.

"That ain't a possum," he said thickly. "That's a bear."

"Larry, back up away from him, real slow," Kyle urged.

"I ain't backin' up from nothin'," Larry said. "I'm scared of no man and no beast. I've been married to Hilda too long."

He unlimbered the lasso and started twirling it sideways. "I'll get him for you, Kyle."

As luck would have it, Larry's lasso landed squarely around the bear's neck. When it did, Larry wrapped the other end of the rope around his forearm and pulled the loop tight.

The bear didn't like it.

A very fast human being can run at about fifteen miles per hour over short distances. A black bear can run at thirty-five miles per hour. Larry was not a very fast human being; he was a very drunk human being.

The bear, on the other hand, was stone-cold sober and apparently had been training for the hundred-meter sprint.

The bear took off at top speed, and since the rope was wrapped around Larry's wrist, so did he. He landed face-first on the ground and bounced like an innertube behind a ski boat as the bear dragged him across the yard.

The bear disappeared around the other end of the building and Kyle, Danny, and I ran the other way to try to keep sight of it and Larry. We shouldn't have bothered. We met the bear in the front yard, charging straight toward us.

We turned back the way we came, and somehow managed to stay ahead of the bear, which was becoming winded from dragging Larry.

"Quick, climb a tree!" Danny yelled.

"Bears can climb!" I yelled back.

"Climb a little tree!" Kyle shouted, pulling himself up into the branches of a Bradford pear. "The limbs will break off with him if he tries to climb. He's too big."

I started climbing another tree. "What about Larry?"

"Larry got hisself into this mess," Danny yelled back from his own tree.

Down below, the bear had stopped, panting, under Kyle's tree. Larry extricated himself from the rope and staggered to his feet.

"Whooo-eee! What a ride!" he whooped.

"Larry! Go inside and call the police. Have them get Fish and Wildlife to send a biologist with a tranquilizer," Kyle instructed.

"No, thanks, beer's fine for me."

"Not for you, stupid, for the bear!"

"Oh! Okay." Larry walked to the back door of Mrs. Lewis' house and knocked loudly. She wouldn't let him in, but informed him she would call the police herself if he didn't get away from her door.

"There's a law against cruelty to animals, you know. I'll not have some drunken hooligans molesting my bear!"

Larry scratched his head then wandered back around the corner of the building, suddenly grasping the gravity of the situation.

"I think I'll just go sit in the car," he said.

When he was gone, Mrs. Lewis poured a large bag of peanuts into a bowl on her back porch and the bear sprang to attention. It ran back to the apartment, grabbed the bowl in its teeth, and then hurried back under Kyle's tree, where it sat down and began eating, one peanut at a time.

"Great, now what are we gonna do?" Kyle asked. "Mrs. Lewis, could you call my emergency number again, please, and tell them the bear has us trapped up here?"

"Well, it serves you right for trying to catch it," she said.

"But, Mrs. Lewis, you called me to come catch it," Kyle reminded her.

"I did not. I just wanted you to see it. You didn't believe me before."

"Mrs. Lewis, would you please call my emergency number?" Kyle pleaded as he adjusted his grip on the tree.

"Well, all right. But they better not bother my bear."

She marched back into the house. We sat in the trees for hours, waiting for someone to arrive, while the bear calmly munched on peanuts. When it ran out of food, it stretched out against Kyle's tree trunk and napped. Periodically, it would wake up, stretch, and stand on its hind legs to sniff in Kyle's direction.

The eastern sky was turning pink, and I was beginning to wonder whether I could stand up in the tree and stay steady enough to pee, when I heard Kyle shout.

"Here they come!"

The shout startled the bear, which had fallen to sleep again. It sat bolt upright, twitched its ears toward the parking lot then ran out of the housing project as fast as its legs would carry it.

It had just disappeared into the bushes when the biologist and a team of conservation workers carrying a ten-foot-long live trap came around the side of the house.

"Where's the bear?" the biologist shouted as we were coming back out of the trees.

"Gone," Kyle told him. "He ran into the bushes when he heard you rattle that trap."

"Where did he go?"

"Over there," Danny said, pointing to the bushes where the bear had disappeared. "Wait! Here he comes again!"

The bushes rustled and a possum stuck its head out then withdrew and disappeared.

The biologist looked at the possum and grinned. "Man, I don't think we brought a big enough trap," he said, starting to laugh. The four men carrying the trap had to set it down to keep from dropping it.

"It's a killer possum, Kyle," one said, sitting down on the trap.

"What I don't understand is after it treed you, why didn't it just climb up and shake you out?" he laughed.

"It ain't shakeout season," another joined in.

Kyle gave them the finger and stomped around the house. Danny and I followed him, leaving Mrs. Lewis to explain that there really was a bear. The last time I looked, she was coming out her back door holding her broom like a club and eyeing the camouflaged trap irritably.

Ordinarily, I would have waited to report on the assault, but my first priority was to find a bathroom and then some breakfast. I also needed time to figure out some way to report the incident without leaving myself open for ridicule.

After two days of thinking, I got lucky and the trappers caught the offending bear. That saved me the embarrassment of reporting the treeing as the lead, but ethics prevented me from ignoring it altogether.

I finally settled on a headline just before the paper went to press.

Game wardens trap bear
after bear traps warden

PART FIVE

LOVE IS A MANY-
SPLINTED THING

In 1958, the Monotones asked the musical question, "Who wrote the book of love?"

Harvey McNeeley didn't write it, but he sure sold a lot of copies.

Harvey was Augusta County's very own version of Larry Flint. His drug store carried every girlie magazine in publication. They were on the top shelf of the magazine rack, out of reach of ten-year-olds, but just a short climb on the bottom shelf for eleven-year-olds.

It became a rite of passage for middle schoolers in Augusta County. When our parents would come to town on the weekend, we'd slip off to Harvey's to "look at the new Case Double-X pocket knives." We all ended up looking at the triple-X pictures.

I spent many Saturdays there with my friends. One of us would keep watch for disapproving grownups while the others looked at the pictures. That worked pretty well until the September morning when Larry Stone got overly excited and failed to keep his eyes where they belonged—namely on the front door. Willie Taylor, our eighth-grade science teacher, walked around the corner of the Hallmark shelf and smack into the middle of our book club.

"What are you boys looking at?" he asked, his bland face carrying the same bland smile it always did.

You'd think a science teacher could figure it out. But, being thirteen at the time, we weren't about to criticize his intelligence. We dropped the magazine and ran. We didn't look back, but I suspect that if we had, we would have seen Mr. Taylor paying Harvey for the magazine and walking out of the store with a plain brown paper bag under his arm.

In spite of Augusta County's location on the Bible Belt, nobody ever said anything to Harvey about his porn collection. Maybe it was because Harvey pretended not to recognize the Baptist elders or the middle-school teachers when they bought each month's edition of *Penthouse*. Or it could have been because most parents were relieved that their sons were getting their information from magazines so they didn't have to have "that talk" with them.

Whatever the reason, Harvey's store was an institution in Augusta County and had been as long as anyone could remember.

I nearly cried the day I picked up Harvey McNeeley's obituary out of the inbox on Anabelle's desk. For a few minutes, standing there with that obituary in my hand, I was back in seventh grade, hiding behind the shelves and trying to look cool at the same time. I was thumbing through the latest edition of *Playboy*, while Danny Vaughn and Kyle Pelphry clamored for their turn, and Larry Stone craned his neck to see if our parents had come into the store.

I was lost in that thought when the bell over the door rang and a gust of wind carried the fragrance of perfume across the counter. I turned to find that the most beautiful woman I'd seen since Miss September, 1976 had walked into *The Journal* office. Her legs curved out of her black spike heels and disappeared into a tantalizingly short black skirt. Where the skirt stopped, her white satin blouse lay flat across her waist then bulged where it ought to bulge. The whole package was topped off with rosy cheeks, red lips, a turned-up nose, and long brown hair that swept down over her shoulders.

I would have waited on her myself, but Anabelle sprang into action before I could regain my senses. More proof that the most efficient employees are not always the best employees to have.

"Good morning. Can I help you?" Anabelle asked.

"I'm not sure. I'm new. I've got some estate notices? From Van Hoose, Van Hoose, and Vanderpool?"

She made the statement as though it were a question, her Deep South accent lending a musical lilt to the words, then she flipped the papers in her hands around to show Anabelle the front.

"You're in the right place," Anabelle assured her. "I'll take those."

"How much do we owe you?"

"We won't know 'til they're set in type. Legal notices are charged by the amount of space they take up. We'll call you when we get it done."

"Who should we ask for?" I asked quickly.

"Georgia. Georgia Burns."

"T.D. Duff," I answered, setting my coffee cup on the counter and stretching out my hand. "I'm the publisher, editor, and so on here."

Georgia reached for my hand, but before I could feel the electric spark of her palm in mine, I felt the hot coffee that she knocked off the counter hit the front of my pants.

Now, I began singing baritone in the church choir when I was fourteen years old, but the coffee induced a note that would have made the best soprano in Augusta County proud. Birds outside in the trees scattered. Dogs across town howled. If I had sustained the note a bit longer, I'm confident that I would have had to replace the windows in the front of the office.

"Ha-ha-ha-HOT!! HOT!"

"Ohmigosh! I'm sorry! I'm sorry!" Georgia yelled as she ran around the end of the counter to help. She had just made the turn and was barreling toward me when she tripped over the rental rug and rammed me in the groin with one of her outstretched hands. Now I had two reasons to lie doubled up on the floor and gasp for breath.

"Oh, God. Are you all right? Say something! I'm so sorry. Can I help?"

"T.D., are you okay?" Anabelle asked, bending over me, too.

I tried to say I was all right, but all I managed was a gurgling sound deep in my throat.

"He needs cold water, quick!" Georgia yelled, standing up abruptly. Her head collided with Anabelle's nose, knocking my fifty-five-year-old receptionist backward onto her desk. When Anabelle stood up, she was howling and trying to staunch the flow of blood from her nose.

"Oh, no! Let me get some tissue," Georgia offered, spinning around to look for some.

"No!" Anabelle and I both yelled at once.

"What?"

"Doe! Thang you, doe!" Anabelle snapped. Her nose interfered with her words, but she got the message across just fine. She clutched her nose with her left hand and pointed to the door with her right.

"Det out before you kill subbody!"

Tears welled up in Georgia's eyes as she turned to go, repeating, "I'm sorry" over and over as she headed for the door. I would have liked to have followed her out and comforted her, but I was in no condition to do it. Besides, I had to work with Anabelle every day and if I had offered sympathy to the woman who had just broken her nose, I would never hear the end of it. I'd have to do it when Anabelle wasn't around.

Georgia trudged out the door sobbing. When Anabelle was sure she was gone, she grabbed a handful of tissue and clamped it over her nose, and then turned back to check on me.

"Are you all ripe?"

"No," I squeaked.

"Good!" she snapped, stalking off toward the restroom.

I took the opportunity to hobble bowlegged into my office, shut the shade on the door, and examine myself for permanent damage. Finding only minor redness and no blisters, I changed into an extra pair of pants I kept in my office and came back out. Anabelle had two pieces of toilet paper billowing out of her nostrils like smoke and a look of scorn on her face.

"Are you burned bad?"

"No, I think I'm okay."

"Well, I guess I'm glad," she said. "But you almost deserved it for ogling that girl the way you were."

"Ogling!? I wasn't..."

"Oh, yes, you were. Ogling. Plain and simple. Couldn't keep your eyes off her boobies. Your mother would be ashamed."

"I...I wasn't ogling," I said, grabbing up the obituaries I had left lying on the counter. "Here, set these. Then send me Harvey's so I can add to it."

I crammed the papers into her hand and stomped back into my office, careful not to let my thighs touch. I didn't have time for this kind of argument. I had a wake to plan.

It had been slow since Bug died, leaving me the newspaper and the responsibility of planning wakes for Augusta County's most prominent residents. I had planned Bug's wake, as he asked, but I had fallen down on my duties otherwise. For one thing, I just wasn't into death like Bug had been. For another, Duff's Wakes just didn't sound as catchy as Wake's Wakes. But Bug Wake had left strict instructions that the tradition of the newspaper publisher planning wakes was to be continued after his death. I had a hard time thinking of anyone more prominent and more deserving of a first-class wake than Harvey McNeeley.

The question was how to have a dignified wake for such an esteemed purveyor of porn. In my mind, I imagined Bug lecturing me from the door of his office, waving his cane in the air.

"Dignity has nothing to do with it! A wake is supposed to be fun. Save the dignity for the funeral."

And with that advice from my mental ghost of Bug Wake, I formulated a plan. I would invite a lot of people, have a eulogy and some light refreshments, and then let the whispered conversation go where it would. No need to mention the magazine rack in a public setting. My buddies and I could snicker and reminisce about that in private. But the fact was Harvey wasn't just a peddler of *Penthouse* and *Playboy*; he was a pharmacist, a Rotarian, and a member in good standing of the Wakefield Shrine Club. He deserved a dignified wake.

I set about making a list of invitees, but everything I did kept Georgia Burns on my mind. When I called Ralph Hobbs, I found out he had moved to Georgia. Brian Woodson lived on Burns Street. Charlie Wills lived on Twin Hills Drive.

I finally gave up trying to plan the wake and started to go to lunch. As I passed the counter, I kicked something on the floor and picked up a woman's wallet.

"Anabelle, is this yours?"

"I've never seen it before," she said. "Oh, no. You don't suppose it's hers, do you? Please tell me it's not. If it is, that means she'll have to come back here again to get it."

I brightened up considerably at the thought then opened the wallet to check for ID. Sure enough, there was Georgia Burns staring back at me, beautiful even in her driver's license mug shot.

"I could take it back to her," I said.

"Why am I not surprised?"

"Because you're a bitter, cynical old maid."

"I'm not an old maid. I'm divorced."

"I wonder why." I held the wallet out to her. "Do you want to take it back?"

"And risk major medical? No, thanks. You can take it. I can see you're dying to ogle some more."

"I wasn't ogling."

"Yes, you were."

"Was not."

"Were so."

I had an overwhelming urge to stick my tongue out at Anabelle, but I suppressed it. Instead, I picked up the phone book.

"I'll call her first," I said, thumbing through the pages to the "V"s. "I can't find Van Hoose, Van Hoose, and Vanderpool."

"It's under 'H,' remember?"

It had momentarily slipped my mind. Van Sr. and Van Jr. thought it sounded more professional to use their full names since Charlie Vanderpool was the third partner. It did sound better than Hoose, Hoose, and Vanderpool.

Georgia offered to come get the wallet herself, but I thought it was best if I took it to her.

"I'll be back soon," I told Anabelle. "Georgia wants to come back over and apologize, too."

"Wait 'til I can run home. I wanna find my son's old catcher's mask."

Georgia was the picture of embarrassment when I walked into the law office. She turned bright red and accepted the wallet with a quick glance downward at my clean pants.

"Is your...are you...all right?" she asked.

"Oh, yeah, I'm fine," I said, being careful not to appear too bowlegged. "Don't worry about that. It could've happened to anybody."

"I don't think so. I'm a klutz."

I couldn't argue with that one, so I changed the subject instead.

"Would you like to go to lunch? Sometime? With me? I'm on my way now."

"Aren't you afraid I'll spill hot coffee on you again? Or spear you with a fork?"

I laughed out loud at that, and shook my head.

"Not in the least. Accidents happen."

And they did.

She didn't spill anything on me at lunch, but she did hit me in the face with the restaurant door. It didn't matter to me, though. It was the most glorious lunch I had ever had, even though I had no idea what I ate and I think the cashier at Kaffey's House lunch counter kept my change. By the time we left, I had Georgia's phone number and a date for the Friday after the wake.

I was stepping high when I walked back into the office, concealing the growing bruise on my cheek and forehead with a baseball cap and a pair of sunglasses.

"Oh, my God. What did she do to you this time?" Anabelle asked.

"Who? What?" I hedged, keeping the right side of my face turned away.

Anabelle got up from her desk and came around the counter, trying to circle around me as I tried to circle away.

"You never wear a cap to work. Did she set your hair on fire? Hit you in the head with a hot waffle iron? Run over you with a lawn mower?"

I broke away from the circular dance and headed for my office.

"Get a life, Anabelle. It's hot out. I'm trying to stay out of the sun."

"Ha! Too late. It's already fried your brains."

I slammed my office door and pulled the shade before I took off my hat and examined my face in the mirror. The bruise was a mottled red and blue, heading toward what was sure to be a uniform purple by morning. I considered giving Anabelle some vacation time until the coloring went away, but finally nixed the idea. I would need her to help get out the word on the wake for Harvey.

I used the intercom to send her down to the VFW club with a deposit for the party room. While she was gone, I left the names and phone numbers of some of the people I hadn't reached on her desk, locked the door, and left for the day. I had already called my closest friends, but I wanted to talk to them in person anyway.

I drove downtown to the funeral home, where I found Danny Vaughn sitting in a rocking chair on the front porch with Kyle Pelphry and Larry Stone. Kyle was still dressed in his game warden's uniform, and Larry was wearing his scrubs, fresh from the X-ray room at Augusta County Methodist Hospital. The three were enjoying a private joke when I walked up to the porch.

"Hey, guys. What's up?"

The three giggled some more and shook their heads.

"It's nothing. We were just talking about Harvey and the magazine rack," Danny explained.

"Those were some good old days, weren't they?" I said.

"Not that old for Harvey," Kyle snickered.

"What are you talking about?"

"You're the reporter feller; ain't you heard?" Larry asked. "Harvey died right there in front of the magazine rack. When they found him, the Pet of the Month was spread out over his face and Miss May was sittin' on his lap."

The three broke up laughing again.

"I knew he died of a heart attack at the drug store. You don't mean he was looking at the magazines when he died? He was just looking, wasn't he?"

Danny waved for me to calm down. "Apparently, he was putting the new magazines on the shelf and taking a quick look through them when his ticker just gave out. He knocked most of 'em off the shelf as he was falling. To make a long story short, he died lying in a whole pile of nekkid women."

"That's how I wanna go," Kyle said wistfully.

I hadn't heard the story, but I was glad they had clued me in.

"Well, guys, we gotta keep this quiet at the wake. Harvey was always real discrete. We've got to be dignified about it."

Larry snickered again. "Don't worry; it'll be a wake that Harvey would be proud of."

"Well, I hope so. I'm really tryin' my best. I've got to..."

"Say, what happened to your face?" Kyle interrupted.

"Yeah. You look like somebody cleaned your clock," Larry put in.

"I ran into a door," I said defensively.

"What was his name?" Danny asked.

"It was a door. You know, hinges, a handle—a door. I was going to lunch with this new legal secretary, Georgia, when. . ."

"Georgia Burns?" Larry asked.

"Yeah. You know her?"

The three glanced at each other and grinned. "Oh, we've seen her," Danny said.

They had the same silly grins plastered on their faces that they had when we were teenagers staring at the centerfolds in Harvey's store.

"Yeah, eat your hearts out." I couldn't help but puff my chest out a little. Georgia was the prettiest woman I'd ever seen in Wakefield or any other part of Augusta County—way prettier than Larry's wife, Hilda, or Danny's live-in, Sherry. Kyle was divorced, but his blue tick hound was prettier than his ex-wife.

Kyle examined his shoes then looked up with a more chastened expression. "So, T.D., you got any nekkid pictures of her?"

"Of course not," I snapped, realizing too late that I had fallen into a middle-school trap.

"You want some?"

They all burst out laughing again, but I was confident in my superiority. All my friends wanted Georgia Burns, but Georgia Burns wanted me. They didn't have a chance.

"Like you'd really get the opportunity to take pictures of her."

"Maybe someday," Kyle sighed.

"Yeah, right. Well, just remember the wake is Friday night at six, and we've got to get out early. I've got a date with Georgia after it's over. Bye-bye, suckers."

Friday was only two days away, so that didn't leave much time to plan. There were flowers to order, a caterer to call, people to invite. I don't know how Bug did it. By the time Anabelle finished, she had to work overtime to get the obituaries and wedding announcements typed.

By Friday, I was as nervous as a cat. Not only was I about to hold the first wake I had planned outside of Bug's, I had a date later with the most beautiful woman who had ever crossed the county line into Augusta County.

"Are you ready?" Anabelle asked, straightening my tie for me and brushing the dust off my shoulder.

"I think so. I mean, the guy's dead. If I mess up the wake, what's he gonna do?"

"I wasn't talking about the wake. I was talking about the date."

"It's not like it's my first date."

"No, just your first one with Miss Firecracker. Now, remember, these days you can't be too careful. Have you got protection?"

"Anabelle!"

"I thought not. Here." She reached under the counter and handed me a batter's helmet and catcher's mask.

Anabelle was still cackling as I shoved through the front door and stalked across the street to my car.

The VFW was across town—a distance of at least a mile—and at rush-hour on a Friday evening, it took almost five minutes to get there. When I arrived, cars were already beginning to line up along the road and the parking lot in back was nearly full. It looked like my first wake outside the "family," so to speak, would be a success after all.

"T.D.!" The call went up from a half-dozen guests as I came through the door. I felt like Norm on the T.V. show *Cheers.*

"Charlie. Ralph. Winston." I dutifully shook hands like a Baptist preacher as I made my way around the room to a booth occupied by Larry, Danny, and Kyle. There were no women at the wake, but that wasn't that surprising, given Harvey's magazine rack and the way he died.

"Howdy, T.D.," Larry said, setting his empty beer can down among the forest of aluminum tree stumps already on the table in front of him.

"Howdy. Gettin' an early start?"

"It's past noon," Kyle noted.

"What's everybody doing here so early? We're not supposed to start 'til six. It's only a quarter til."

"I guess everybody wanted to see what's coming off," Danny said.

Larry spewed beer out his nose.

"Are you all right? What happened?"

"He's got hiccups," Kyle said, slapping him hard on the back.

Danny slapped a stack of napkins over Larry's nose and mouth. "Must have caused him to get strangled."

"Well, be careful, buddy. I guess I better say a few words."

"Let me introduce you," Danny said, jumping up and walking to the microphone.

"Gentlemen, gentlemen." Danny tapped the microphone for attention and the room quieted down.

"You all know why we're here tonight." The crowd broke out in applause. "So without any further adieu, I'd like to introduce our host for this wake, T.D. Duff."

The crowd applauded politely as I stepped to the edge of the stage.

"We're gathered here to pay our last respects to Harvey McNeeley: businessman, Shriner, Rotarian, and a true citizen of Wakefield.

"Harvey McNeeley was a good man. He worked tirelessly on the crippled children's hospital with the Shriners, the..."

Someone shouted something from the audience that I took to be "amen," and I forged ahead into Harvey's many accomplishments with the Shrine Club and the Rotary. I'd seen Bug do this kind of thing numerous times, but somehow I felt like I just wasn't doing something right. The audience apparently felt differently. Every time I'd hit a point about Harvey's life, a whoop would go up somewhere in the crowd. When I talked about his trip to Nepal with the Rotary Club, Bill Hart whistled so loudly my ears rang. When I talked about his efforts to raise money for eyeglasses for the poor, Charlie Wills climbed onto the table and yelled, "Yee-haw!"

I had the strange feeling that something was going on that I couldn't see, and I didn't really trust Larry, who was hanging around behind me, holding on to the stage curtain. I was pretty sure he was up to something, but for the life of me, I couldn't figure out what he could be doing that would draw such a lively reaction from the crowd. After five minutes, my nerves got the best of me and I signed off.

"I know you all are pretty broken up about Harvey, so I'll leave it at that and we can get on with the celebration," I said.

A roar went up from the crowd and someone bumped into me. I turned to find Danny and Kyle had come through the curtains to join Larry, who took the microphone and burped into it.

"Every time I think about Harvey, I think about Miss November, 1976. Man, did she ever have a pair of tits…"

I made a grab for the microphone, but Larry tossed it to Danny and stumbled down the steps on the other side of the stage.

"She sure did, Larry. Now, gentlemen! For your entertainment, and in fond remembrance of wonderful man, and of Miss November, we have found a way to pay fitting tribute to Harvey McNeeley's life's work. We have a new resident in Wakefield, who was near and dear to Harvey's…heart."

I suddenly got a sick feeling in the pit of my stomach. Kyle grinned and the sick feeling got worse. Something terrible was about to happen and I had to stop it.

Danny dodged around Kyle and ran to the other side of the stage as I tried to catch him.

"Our special guest never knew Harvey, but I'm sure Harvey knew her. Straight from the pages of *Easy Rider* and *The Girls of the Southeastern Conference*…"

Danny made another turn around the stage as I lunged after him, trying to get within reach of the microphone.

"Miss Pan Head and Miss I Felta Delta herself…Georgia Burns!"

Kyle grabbed the rope that opened the curtain, and there she was. My date for the evening was standing center stage on a raised platform and she wasn't dressed for her day job at Van Hoose, Van Hoose, and Vanderpool anymore. In fact, she was barely dressed at all. Her bottom half was hidden behind a giant feather fan but her top half was covered only by two homemade pasties emblazoned with Harvey McNeeley's smiling face. The twins were staring me in each eye.

That's when I got flashed again—by Kyle's Polaroid camera.

Larry had returned to the stage and was staring open-mouthed at Georgia as Danny reached out a hand to help her down from the platform onto the main stage. In planning the whole night, Danny, Larry, and Kyle apparently had focused solely on Georgia Burns' physical attributes, and had either ignored or overlooked her physical awkwardness.

Had they been aware of her clumsiness, they might have rethought the idea of placing her on a sixteen-inch pedestal.

As one long, tanned leg stepped down from the riser, her shoe heel caught on the microphone cord trailing out of Danny's hand, causing her to pitch forward and knock me clear off the stage.

I landed flat on my back. Georgia landed flat on my front.

Kyle immediately snapped more pictures.

The audience went wild.

I know I should have been embarrassed, but for some reason I barely noticed the crowd. All I saw was Georgia's lips poised inches above mine. I finally regained my composure enough to roll her off me and sit up. Larry, Kyle, and Danny had suddenly disappeared, but the crowd of "mourners" was still there, applauding and panting at Georgia, who stood proudly in front of the stage, waving and blowing kisses.

"Everybody out!"

I delivered the ultimatum as forcefully as possible, but no one was listening. Georgia and the twin Harveys were still smiling.

I tried one more time and got the same result as before. As badly as I hated to do it, this called for desperate measures. I grabbed a tablecloth off the nearest table, wrapped it around Georgia, and then picked up the microphone.

"Get out!"

"Aw, T.D., whaddaya wanna do that for?" Bill McQueen whined.

"Yeah, the wake's just startin' to liven up," Tommy Dunn chimed in.

"Out. The party's over. Goodbye."

I shoved the microphone back into the stand and went to the door, holding it open for the grumbling revelers. I never did see Danny, Kyle, and Larry. When the last person left, I locked the door and thumped my head against it. It didn't help and it hurt like hell.

"I guess that means our date is off?"

I hadn't realized that Georgia was still there. I pondered the question for a long moment. I could go out with the woman who had just appeared 98 percent naked in front of fifty of my closest friends and be laughed at—maybe. Or maybe I would be envied. There was certainly a lot for them to be envious of. Or I could refuse to go out with her and definitely be laughed at.

"You mean you still want to go out?"

"Well, I'm not sure you want to be seen with me now, but..."

I finally turned around and looked at Georgia. She really was a beautiful woman, and she looked genuinely sorry for the scene.

"Who's going to fault me for being seen with someone as beautiful as you?"

Georgia smiled and looked around the room.

"You know, there's plenty of food here." She picked up a lit candle from the table. "We could have a candlelight dinner."

My visions of a pleasant dinner gave way to visions of burning hair. I took the candle out of Georgia's hand, blew it out, and set it back on the table.

"Dinner sounds good. By the way, how did you happen to end up...uh... here? Tonight."

"Oh, Danny asked me. I made a personal appearance at a funeral director's convention last fall. He recognized me when I moved here and asked me if I would come out tonight. It was kind of a last-minute thing."

"Danny's a real card."

"I hate that you didn't like it. Danny said you'd get a real kick out of it."

"That's okay. I'm sure Danny got a kick out of it. Or he will later."

"Well, let's just forget it and talk about something else. Why don't you get us something to drink while I get dressed? I'll help you clean this place up after we eat."

Georgia dropped her tablecloth and walked away, completely oblivious of the fact that her present outfit could have been used for a sling shot and two coasters. I wasn't happy about the spectacle Danny's little joke had made of the wake, but I had to be somewhat grateful to him as well.

"Well?? Tell me about it! What happened last night?" Anabelle's voice sounded like a hammer on a tin dishpan over the telephone.

I was kicked back on the balcony of my apartment, taking in the Saturday morning sun and sipping tomato juice.

"Anabelle! You don't think I'd kiss and tell, do you?"

"Kiss and... I'm not interested in your date."

"Oh, you mean the wake." My mind was racing to come up with a story to tell, but I was wasting my time.

"I know all about Miss Hoochie Coochie. I mean the fire!"

"What fire?"

"Some reporter you are. I mean the fire at the VFW."

"Oh, come on, Anabelle. Do you really expect me to believe that? Georgia and I were there way after everybody else left, cleaning the joint up."

"Georgia was there, huh? Well, that explains it. I can see the headline now: 'Georgia Burns VFW.'"

I suddenly had an awful feeling that Anabelle wasn't joking. I tried to remember if we had blown out all the candles when we left, but I couldn't for the life of me. Georgia had been the last one out the door. Given her proclivity for catastrophe, it was entirely possible that she had played the role of Mrs. O'Leary's cow at the VFW.

I hung up on Anabelle without saying goodbye and tried to remember if I had heard any sirens after I got home. I couldn't recall if there had been a siren or not. Usually my ears are tuned in for that sound. The puzzle would have to remain a puzzle, at least until after breakfast.

Georgia may have indeed burned the VFW, but she had made my eggs over easy and they were getting cold.

PART SIX

SLEEPING DOGS

A breeze tickled the hairs on the back of Danny Vaughn's balding head and the sky was the same color blue as, well, as blue as...*a Robin's egg*, Danny thought. He silently thanked the birds that were singing on the hedge to the left of the big, roll-up door for reminding him of the comparison. The temperature hovered around eighty-four degrees and the fragrance of mimosa drifted over the parking lot. The only way it could get better was if he were pulling a prank on his best friend, T.D. Duff.

The last one had been a dandy. Danny laughed to himself as he thought of the look on T.D.'s face when he found out his new girlfriend was a nude magazine model. The revelation in itself wasn't so funny, but her personal appearance in pasties and a g-string in front of a roomful of attendees at a wake hosted by T.D. couldn't be topped. But Danny would, of course, try to top it the next time a golden opportunity presented itself.

But for now he had to work. *Oh, what the hell?* Danny thought. *There's even joy to be found in work.*

He chuckled at his own play on words as he opened the back doors of the black Suburban and pulled out the gurney that carried the last worldly remains of Joy Henderson. He quickly sobered his attitude and wheeled the gurney through the door and down the ramp to the stone-walled basement, carefully negotiating the turn into the embalming room.

"Hey! Danny! You down there yet?" a voice yelled from the top of the ramp that led to the viewing room upstairs.

"Yeah!" he yelled back, skillfully pulling the gurney up beside the worn porcelain embalming table and locking the wheels.

"You got a customer up here," Milton Lee yelled back from upstairs.

Danny sighed. Milton was a good assistant in a lot of ways. When it came to making a corpse look like it was going to sit right up in the casket, Milton was an artist. But give him a live customer and he was lost. Since he strained his back lifting a particularly heavy corpse onto the embalming table, he was pretty much lost all the time. At least he had driven the hearse to bring the body here, even if Danny did have to unload it.

"I'm kinda busy down here, Milt. Can Sherry or you take care of them?" Danny asked loudly.

"Sherry's gone to the dentist."

"I forgot. Can you take care of them?"

There was a long pause as Milton considered the request.

"No."

Danny sighed and took off the surgical apron he had just put on.

"Could you come down here, then?"

There was another long pause.

"Okay," Milton said reluctantly.

Danny made his way upstairs as Milton came down. It was only a payment on pre-need arrangements, so in five minutes he was back in the embalming room. By the time he got there, Milton had already placed Joy Henderson on the embalming table and removed her clothes. Joy was twenty-eight years old, a busty brunette with long eyelashes and perfect makeup. She had moved to town a month before and she had worked in the Shoney's restaurant on the old bypass until the night before.

Joy roomed with T.D.'s girlfriend, Georgia Burns. Georgia had called the police when Joy didn't come home, but the Wakefield Police, knowing Joy's looks and Georgia's background as a nude model, had laughed off the report. If she didn't come home, it was probably because she went home with somebody else.

As it turned out, Georgia Burns had been right. Joy's coworkers found her when they opened up the next morning, huddled in a corner of the walk-in freezer, deader than a door nail. She apparently stayed late to put away some frozen foods and got locked in the freezer. Milton had gotten the call from the coroner and picked up the body.

The Body. That was appropriate. He shook his head sadly. *Damn shame*, he thought, his eyes settling on her ample breasts. *That freezer must have been really cold*, Danny thought.

Danny dismissed the thought from his head and turned on the radio. It was already set to his favorite oldies station and Danny whistled along with The Beatles as he placed the gurney in its usual parking spot outside the door and pulled little square, pink bottles of Metaflow and Metasyn from the wire rack beside the embalming table.

He was pouring the fluids into the foot-high glass jar on the embalming pump when Milton yelled again.

"What, Milton?"

"You got somebody else up here that needs to talk to you!"

Danny opened his mouth to speak, but thought better of it. He sat the half-used bottle of Metasyn down between Joy Henderson's perfectly pedicured feet, stripped off his gloves and apron again, and went back upstairs.

This time it was the UPS driver. When Danny walked into the office, Milton was eyeing the package doubtfully and rubbing his back.

"You know I ain't supposed to lift anything."

"You lifted that body just now. She weighs a hell of a lot more than this package."

Milton blushed and stuttered. "I hurt my back again doing it."

Danny put the ten-pound package on the filing cabinet, gave Milton a withering look, and went back to the embalming room. The bottle of Metasyn had fallen off the table and the pink fluid, a 20-percent solution of formaldehyde, was slowly spreading across the painted concrete floor. Danny sighed, and grabbed a mop from the corner.

When he turned around, Joy Henderson was sitting straight up on the embalming table, looking slowly around the room.

Danny jumped a foot off the floor, fumbled the mop, then regained his composure and slowly approached the table.

"Hello," he said politely.

"Where am I?" Joy asked, turning her pretty head to take in the tangle of rubber hoses on the shelf above the table and the stainless-steel surgical instruments in the tray beside her.

Danny pursed his lips thoughtfully before replying.

"You, uh, you're in the, uh, funeral home," he said gently.

Joy's mouth dropped open, her eyes rolled back, and she passed out.

Danny wasted no time.

"Milton!" he screamed.

No answer.

"Milton! Get down here! Bring the phone! Quick, damn it!"

Milton ran into the room with the cordless phone just as Danny laid his ear between Joy's breasts to listen for a heartbeat.

"Damn, Danny," Milton gasped.

Danny jumped up involuntarily. "You idiot, she's alive," Danny snapped. "At least she was a minute ago. We gotta do CPR. You start and let me have the phone."

Milton clutched the phone to the front of his starched white shirt and backed up. "I don't know nothin' about CPR, boss. I just work with 'em after they're dead."

"She is dead, damn it, or she wouldn't need CPR!"

"I told you, I don't know CPR!"

"Don't just stand there...call somebody," Danny ordered.

Milton dialed a number and stepped out into the hall.

Danny stuck his ear back between Joy's breasts and found a heartbeat. It seemed strong, but since he was used to dealing with people with no heartbeat, he really had nothing to compare it to. Her body was warm, however. He held Joy's hand and tried to wake her up, but her eyes remained closed. It seemed like hours before Walter Strait walked through the door of the embalming room, eating a sandwich.

"He's here," Milton announced.

"What do you mean he's here?"

"You told me to call somebody, so I called Walter."

"You called the coroner?" Danny gasped. "I meant call an ambulance!"

"Oh!" Milton exclaimed, retreating into the hallway again.

"Why do you need an ambulance?" Walter asked innocently. "She's dead. I pronounced her myself. Damn shame, too. Did you ever see tits like that in all your born days?"

Danny glared at Walter, but, somewhat relieved that there was a pulse, he resisted the urge to smack him.

"Check again, you putz. She's alive," Danny said.

"No, she's not," Walter said, taking a bite of his egg salad sandwich.

"Yes, she is."

"Are you sure?"

Danny hung his head. "She sat up and spoke to me, Walter. I'm pretty damn sure that means she's alive."

Walter checked her pulse then bit his lip. "Did you check her rectal temp?"

Danny shook his head in disbelief. "Did I what?"

"Check her rectal temp. You see, once it drops below a certain level, it's a pretty good indicator that they're dead. I got a thermometer, see?" He pulled a thermometer from his shirt pocket and held it up for Danny to see.

Danny looked at him silently, his mouth open in disbelief. He was still trying to think of something to say when Tommy Dunn and Bill McQueen, paramedics for the Wakefield Volunteer Fire Department, rushed through the door.

"What's wrong? Who needs an ambulance?" Bill asked.

"She does," Danny said, relieved. "You've got to get her to the hospital, quick."

"She's dead," the medic said flatly. "It's a shame, too. Will you look at those tits?"

Danny shivered in rage.

"She's alive, damn it, and, yes, I've seen her tits. Now check her pulse or take her blood pressure or do whatever it is paramedics are supposed to do. And take her to the hospital!" he bellowed.

Bill approached the table with a condescending smile and picked up Joy's wrist.

"Who are you?" she asked groggily.

Bill jumped in surprise, dropped Joy's hand, and fell over backwards.

"Shit!" Danny yelped, peering over the table at the prostrate body of the medic.

Walter knelt beside the man and felt of his neck.

"I think he's dead," Walter said.

"What do you mean he's dead?" Danny asked in horror. "I can't have people dying in my embalming room."

"Well, he's dead," Walter replied, still eating his sandwich and staring at Joy's chest.

"I want a second opinion!"

"Gimme back my thermometer, then."

Brian Woodson knelt down beside his partner and felt his neck then his wrist. Tears welled up in the young man's eyes.

"Bill's dead," he said, his face contorting with grief.

"Who are you people? Where are my clothes?" Joy demanded.

"I told you he was dead," Walter snapped.

Danny grabbed a bottle of Metaflow off the rack and shoved it into Walter's hands.

"Fine. You embalm him." He yanked off his gloves and threw them in the trash, pulled off his apron and handed it to Joy to cover herself, and then stormed out of the room.

T.D. Duff and Georgia sat together in the back booth of the Eight Ball Bar when Danny came through the door and went straight for the bar. He downed his third shot of Jim Beam in under a minute and avoided all contact with everyone around him. Larry Stone and Kyle Pelphry tried to get him to sit at their table, but Danny refused their company. He sat alone, his back to the front door and his eyes focused firmly on the bar top. He didn't even notice when Joy slipped in through the back door and scooted into the booth across from T.D. and Georgia. She pulled a menu up in front of her face, took out a compact, and began wiping the eyeshadow from her blue-tinted lips.

"What's he doing?"

"Getting drunk," Georgia said.

"When you two get even, you really get even. When are you gonna tell him it was all a set-up?"

"In a little while. I'm gonna let him get good and drunk first," T.D. said.

Bill McQueen popped through the door and slid into the seat beside Joy, his face hidden by sunglasses and a cap. "Can I come back to life yet?"

"Not yet. Keep your hat on."

Danny had half of his fourth glass of bourbon left when Sgt. Ira Ripley of the Wakefield Police Department came in for a drink at the end of his shift and sat down on the next stool.

"Hey, Danny Boy, how's it hangin'?"

Danny grunted a reply and continued to sip his bourbon.

"Hell of a day, huh, Danny?"

Getting no reply, Ira ordered a beer and pushed his gun belt down under his spreading gut to a more comfortable position.

"First thing I heard when I came in this morning was about that Joy chick's death. What a thing. Only twenty-eight years old. Damn shame to die that young. Nice girl, too. I used to eat lunch there just to look at her tits," Ira reminisced.

Danny shut his eyes and drained his glass. He set it back on the bar and pulled out some bills, waving them at Frank, the bartender, before laying the money on the bar.

"Hey, tell me something, Danny. Just between me and you. I know they sent her over to your funeral home. Did you, uh," Ira looked around furtively and lowered his voice. "Did you, like, touch 'em and see if they was real?"

Danny looked Ira in the eye then punched him square in the face, knocking him off the bar stool onto his back. Danny slowly tucked his shirttail back into his pants and wiped the thin strand of hair that covered his bald spot back into place.

"He knocked him out cold!" Larry muttered in disbelief.

"Cold, hell! I think he's dead," Kyle said.

"Take my word for it," Danny said. "If he's cold, he's dead."

He took the thermometer Walter Strait had shoved at him out of his shirt pocket and laid it down on the table between the two gossips.

"Here, check for yourself," he said, then hitched his pants up, shoved his glasses back on his nose, and staggered out the door for home.

PART SEVEN

WAKEFIELD'S MOST WANTED

Wakefield's police department consists of fourteen men, six cars, and a 1972 Army surplus pickup truck. The Augusta County Sheriff's Department is even smaller, with just three deputies, two of whom had to buy their own cruisers. But despite the small size of the police departments, the people of Augusta County feel completely safe. It's not that the police here always get their man; it's just that there's rarely a man to get.

The lack of crime doesn't mean that the police around Wakefield are complacent. They're positively catatonic.

And catatonic was something that Captain G.W. Fitzhugh of the state police could not tolerate in a law enforcement officer. That's why he called his special anti-crime meeting at the Ponderosa Steak House last April and invited every police officer in the county to attend. He also invited every member of the press, which is why I went. I am every member of the press in Augusta County.

For those of you who haven't met me, I'm T.D. Duff—the publisher, editor, reporter, photographer, advertising manager, and pretty much everything else at *The Wakefield Journal.* I inherited this rag when Bug Wake, the previous owner, died, leaving me with a mountain of debt and a molehill of news. Considering the lack of news, an anti-crime meeting looked as exciting as an expedition up Mount McKinley.

The Ponderosa sits on a knoll in a little shopping center on the outskirts of town. It's the only restaurant in a cluster of buildings that includes a Walgreen's and a Super Dollar. If this were a city, the Ponderosa would be on an out-parcel at the mall, but in a town like Wakefield, everything's an out-parcel. The parking lot circles the building and at the moment it was filled with mismatched sheriff's cars, the entire city police motor pool, and five shiny gray state police cars, all identical in make, model, color, and the arrangement of antennae on the trunks.

I had to park my Camaro beside a pickup full of concrete blocks in front of the Walgreen's. Lee Roy Holder popped through the door of the drug store with a preoccupied look on his face and a plastic bag in his hand, nearly bowling me over as I stepped onto the sidewalk.

He flashed me a grin through his tangled blond beard. One tooth was missing and his mullet looked like it had been caught in a tornado.

"Wha'd'ya know, T.D.?"

"All on me, Lee Roy. What's up?"

Lee Roy's lips twisted into a more conspiratorial grin and he glanced from side to side.

"Not a thing, far as you know." He winked at me, chuckled, and climbed into the pickup that I had parked beside.

I had known Lee Roy since grade school, and we often ran in the same circles, but Lee Roy was different. While I would go to a party and drink a couple beers, he would go and drink a couple of cases. He was also not averse to taking a toke in public, or brawling in the parking lot of the VFW. More than one husband would love to get his hands on Lee Roy because more than one wife had. It wasn't that Lee Roy was anything much to look at; he was just one of those bad boys that seemed to attract women like a belly button attracts lint.

Lee Roy stuck his head out the window as I started across the parking lot.

"You gonna eat over at the Ponderosa?"

I nodded and walked backward toward the restaurant, trying to look like I was in a big hurry. I liked Lee Roy all right, but I didn't really want him inviting himself to lunch with me. I was worried for nothing.

"Tell that state po-lice captain howdy for me," he said, grinning.

Lee Roy wasn't exactly on the state police's Christmas list, but I told him I'd pass it along and went on to Ponderosa.

Other than police, there was the usual crowd of Buick and Oldsmobile drivers, and a couple of Chryslers. The meeting was in the private dining room in back, and I was early enough to catch the solemn handshaking ritual before it started.

Capt. Fitzhugh was a serious man, even for a state trooper. He was about fifty, tall, and square by both physical and mental standards. His hawkish eyes never stopped moving and his lips never smiled when he grabbed my hand in his paw and squeezed. Fitzhugh was the kind of cop who gave cops a bad name. Not that he was dishonest. If anything, he was too honest. He didn't give anyone a break for any reason. He had personally given me a ticket for driving sixty miles an hour in a fifty-five zone on my way to an accident, and he had impressed on his troopers the importance of making sure no one in the region had a burned-out headlight or forgot to use their turn signals.

When the introductions were made and everyone sat down at the tables, Fitzhugh walked to the podium set up at the end of the room and cast a stern gaze over the assembled peace officers. The room became silent immediately. Troopers sat at attention and deputies quickly tried to imitate their ramrod posture. Only Sheriff Charlie Stewart seemed unimpressed, continuing to eat his salad and crunch loudly on his croutons. Fitzhugh glared at him, but Charlie ignored him and kept eating.

"Gentlemen, I called you all here today to discuss the deplorable state of lawlessness we are witnessing in Augusta County," Fitzhugh began.

Deputies and city patrolmen looked at each other askance, but Fitzhugh continued.

"I have last month's crime statistics with me today and it is a very...serious... situation. Three burglaries, twelve DUIs, two trespasses, and eighty-four traffic offenses. All but six of these offenses were handled by the state police."

Charlie Stewart picked his teeth, and went back to chewing. Deputies, taking a cue from their boss, began to slump again and city police started picking at their food.

Fitzhugh continued his harangue at local officers for fifteen minutes before making a rousing call to arms and an assertion of brotherly forgiveness for his local counterparts.

He ended with his grand idea in crime fighting: the most-wanted list.

I thought the sheriff was going to choke on his sirloin at that one. He was still chuckling and sort of purple when the captain left the podium and came to sit beside me, making the trooper who had been there find another chair.

"I hope you got all of that and will report it accurately, Mr. Duff," Fitzhugh growled.

"I always do, Mr. Fitzhugh."

"Captain Fitzhugh."

"Sorry."

The meal was a tense affair. Deputies and troopers who were normally on friendly terms kept their mouths shut. I wolfed down my hot bar meal and excused myself, unable to sit beside the captain any longer. I had cleared the outside door and was halfway across the parking lot before I realized something was wrong.

All of the city and county patrol cars were fine, but the state police cars were definitely not fine.

The wheels were missing from all five.

Each car sat on concrete blocks and each had the same legend written across its windshield in white shoe polish: "Lee Roy Wuz Here."

❧

Lee Roy had a way of livening things up, and he had certainly livened things up this time. The meeting had been on Monday morning, and by the time I put the paper to bed on Monday night, Captain Fitzhugh was already screaming for the sheriff to make Lee Roy Holder the most-wanted man in Augusta County.

Since Charlie Stewart didn't much care for Captain G.W. Fitzhugh, it didn't look as though that was going to happen. The paper went to press with a picture of the police cars, and another of Fitzhugh in a fit of apoplexy when he came outside and saw them. The story made a big deal of the fact that the wheels had been stolen off the police cars during an anti-crime meeting, told of Fitzhugh's call for naming Lee Roy as the county's most-wanted man, and included Charlie Stewart's well-reasoned quotation that a most-wanted list for Augusta County would be the shortest list in history.

It was plain that Sheriff Charlie Stewart had no intention of mounting a manhunt for Lee Roy Holder. But as the week progressed, the Case of the Purloined Pirellis became something that was harder and harder for the Augusta County sheriff to ignore.

An hour after the paper came out Tuesday morning, one state police-issue car tire was hanging on the saber of Stonewall Jackson's statue in the town square. Two days later, another one was floating in the fountain in front of the courthouse. The next Monday, a tire was tied with a red ribbon and leaned against the front door of the sheriff's department.

"T.D., you ain't gonna put a pitcher of that tire in the paper, are you?" Charlie asked, fiddling with his letter opener.

"Charlie, you know I have to. Lee Roy stealing the tires off of Captain Fitzhugh's cruiser is the biggest joke, er, news in the county. Hell, you thought it was as funny as anybody."

Charlie grinned in spite of himself then cleared his throat and got serious.

"Look, T.D., I've helped you out more times than I can count. What about last month when you had that Joy girl fake being dead so you could prank Danny Vaughn over at the funeral home? I talked to Chief Myers and kept him from arresting Danny for decking Ira Ripley. That ought to be worth something."

"Yeah, but Charlie, you never liked Ira Ripley anyway. You fired him for being a drunk. Besides, this picture only makes Fitzhugh and the state boys look bad. Since when have you cared what Fitzhugh thinks?"

"Since he's been pressuring the county supervisors to cut my budget. The damn tightwads are always lookin' for a way to save money, and Fitzhugh's showin' them how to do it. When I wouldn't make Lee Roy Holder our most wanted, Fitzhugh took his little charts and graphs to the supervisors and showed them how many arrests his troopers made compared to us."

I had visions of Charlie's department going down the drain, giving Fitzhugh another excuse to increase patrols.

"What did you do?"

"What else could I do?" He handed a wanted poster across the desk with a grainy blow-up of Lee Roy's mug shot.

I was on the phone with my girlfriend, Georgia, the next day when the line suddenly went dead. I turned my swivel chair around to find Capt. Fitzhugh leaning across my desk with his finger on the cut-off button of the telephone.

"Excuse me?" I snapped.

"We need to have a conversation, Mr. Duff."

"I was already having a conversation, Captain."

Fitzhugh slapped a copy of that week's newspaper down on my desk and jammed a blunt forefinger down on the photograph on page five. It was a sub-mitted photo of the graduating class of nurses from the vocational school.

"How do you explain this?"

I glanced at the photo, juxtaposed next to a hunting story.

"Whitetail deer population increases?" I offered.

Fitzhugh sneered and pointed to a face in the back row of the nurses. Lee Roy Holder grinned at the lens over the shoulder of a busty young nurse.

"I didn't know Lee Roy was in nursing school."

"He's not in nursing school. I checked. But he's in your newspaper the same day that his wanted poster is on your front page. Why didn't you call us when you took this?"

"I didn't take this; it was submitted. Not that I would have called you anyway, but..."

Fitzhugh snatched up the paper.

"I'll be watching you, Duff."

The captain stomped out of my office and out of the newspaper office. A better man would have forgotten about the whole thing, but I never claimed to be a better man.

The next week's newspaper carried a front-page photo of the Founder's Day celebration. Lee Roy sat right behind the mayor in the photograph, smiling for the camera.

Captain Fitzhugh stopped by the office to complain again, but I gave him the standard First Amendment speech then left him standing in front of Anabelle's reception desk and went to lunch.

"T.D., if you ever leave me alone with that insufferable son-of-a-bitch again, I'll quit," she informed me when I got back from lunch.

"But, Anabelle, I thought you'd like him. He's got a steady job; he's an upstanding citizen. He's single, too."

"Because nobody would have him," she snorted. "I'm warning you T.D.: if that man comes in here again, I'm calling the police."

"He is the police."

"I won't be calling them to get him; I'll be turning myself in for killing you."

The next week we carried a picture on the sports page of the celebration after the high school basketball team's win at the state tournament. Lee Roy was dancing around center court with a dozen female fans.

The day the paper came out, Anabelle sat on the edge of her seat, ready to disappear if the captain pulled up outside. Fortunately for me, he only called on the phone. I laid the receiver on my desk while I made coffee and waited for him to run out of steam then politely told him I couldn't help him and hung up. I figured if I kept ignoring his demands long enough, he'd leave me alone, so the next week Lee Roy's escapades got the best play ever. I wrote a front-page, in-depth profile of him, complete with an environmental portrait of Wakefield's most wanted sitting on a pile of tires.

Captain Fitzhugh was rapidly becoming the laughing stock of Augusta County, and Lee Roy Holder was a folk hero. The VFW named him man of the year and the Wakefield Women's Club started a legal defense fund for him.

"T.D., this Lee Roy Holder business has got to stop," Charlie Stewart said. We were having lunch together at McNeeley's Drug Store. I normally sit at the counter, but the sheriff asked me to join him in a booth at the back when I came in.

"What do you mean?"

"You know what I mean. We're supposed to be looking for Lee Roy and you've got his picture all over the paper. It makes us look bad."

"I don't think it makes you look bad."

Charlie's mouth opened, but he stopped before he could say anything. He turned the thought over in his head.

"Okay, so it makes Fitzhugh look bad. I thought you newspaper types were supposed to be unbiased."

"I thought people were supposed to knock before they come into someone else's office."

"What?"

"Nevermind. Did you watch the Braves and the Yankees last night?" I said, attempting to change the subject.

I downed the last bite of my club sandwich and tossed a dollar bill on the table.

"Gotta go, Charlie. I'll see you around."

"Wait a minute. What about the pictures?"

"I just cover the news, Charlie. I can't pretend like things don't happen... can't keep stories and pictures out of the paper."

I left before Charlie could say anything else, stopping at the counter just long enough to pay my check.

Of course, Sheriff Charlie Stewart was right: reporters were supposed to be unbiased. But I was also the editor of *The Wakefield Journal*, and editors are supposed to take positions on matters of public importance. I didn't think much more about it after that, but I did do Charlie a favor. There were no pictures of Lee Roy Holder in the paper the next week. However, there was a story about the fifteen wheels and tires that were still missing being stacked up in front of the sheriff's office. A note was attached, apologizing to Charlie and the rest of the sheriff's department for embarrassing them, and explaining that his only bad feelings were toward the state police.

"Since captin fitzhue has been here, the state police has give me 8 tickets. I can't pay my child support or buy food if I have to keep paying fines. Sheriff Stewart has always been good to me. When he arrests me, he keeps me in jail till I sober up and then he sends me home. He don't take all my money and make my children starve."

It was signed, "Lee Roy wuz here."

There was also a photo of Charlie's deputies unloading the tires from a truck in front of the state police barracks. Captain Fitzhugh, however, was unmoved by the apology. He had insisted I call him before I put anything else in the paper, so I did and quoted his tirade about the need for Lee Roy to pay for his crimes.

The legal defense fund created by the Women's Club had grown to more than five hundred dollars by the morning the newspaper came out. It had doubled by the next day as the news spread that Lee Roy had stolen the tires to protect his children. It didn't matter that Lee Roy had never been married or that no one had ever proved that the children people suspected him of fathering were really his. After all, at least two belonged to women who were already married.

"T.D.! Man, you're my hero!"

Lee Roy smacked me on the back so hard I spilled beer all over my shoes. I had just filled a cup out of the keg at the annual Shriners' Charity Pig Roast when Lee Roy slipped up behind me.

"Aw hell, Lee Roy, you're the only hero in Augusta County these days," I said, wiping beer off my shirt front.

"I know, but you had a little bit to do with it. Them ladies at the Women's Club have raised enough money to hire a first-class lawyer if I ever need one. There wasn't but two of 'em would even give me the time a-day before, and then they'd scrunch down in my truck seat to keep folks from seein' us."

"Yeah, well, Lee Roy, don't count on needing a lawyer. Fitzhugh is transferring to the other end of the state, and the sheriff will probably take you off that most-wanted list once he's gone."

"Take me off?? That list is the best thing that ever happened to me! Women love outlaws. I'm Wakefield's most-wanted man since that list come out."

"Lee Roy, you've always been an outlaw, but this is serious. You know, wanted posters, manhunts? Handcuffs?" I looked for some sign of understanding, but saw none. "You shouldn't even be here. The state boys are having a road check outside the front gate."

"I seen 'em when I came in. Looked straight at me," a grin passed over Lee Roy's face again. "Did you bring your camera with you, Picture Man?"

"Yeah, it's in the car. Why?"

"Nothin', I just thought you might want to put another picture of me in the paper."

Lee Roy wandered off through the crowd, leaving me a little nervous about what he had in mind. A half-hour later, my cell phone rang.

"That you, T.D.?"

"Yes, this is T.D. Who is this? Lee Roy?"

"T.D., I been thinkin' about what you said, and I just can't let 'em take me off the most-wanted list."

"Lee Roy, what are you thinking?"

"You better get up here to the gate if you wanna find out. And bring your camera."

I ran back through the crowd to my car and then up the driveway from the field where the pig roast was being held. When I reached the highway, the state police and a couple of deputies were stopping cars in both directions and checking drivers' licenses. Captain Fitzhugh himself was standing in the middle of the highway with a flashlight directing traffic. Lee Roy was nowhere in sight at first, but then I saw movement on the opposite side of the highway.

Lee Roy slipped out of the darkness beside the road and waved at me. He grinned widely then eased open the driver's door of Captain Fitzhugh's cruiser.

"Lee R...!" I cut myself off before I could finish and ducked down behind the guardrail. One of the troopers looked my way then turned back to the driver he had stopped. I raised my head just enough to see Lee Roy hold one finger to his lips to shush me. I was helpless to stop him. I watched in horror as Lee Roy twisted the steering wheel all the way to the left and then bent over in the seat as though he were looking for something. I realized what it was a second later when the siren began to wail.

Troopers and deputies nearly jumped out of their skins as Lee Roy lit up the tires on the Crown Victoria. Gravel flew and white smoke boiled as the cruiser did doughnuts in the middle of the highway.

With nothing else to do, I started snapping pictures. Lee Roy stuck his arm out the window and gave Fitzhugh the bird.

Suddenly, the car straightened out and barreled back toward Wakefield. Behind it, a long string of beer cans hooked to the bumper rattled on the asphalt. Police scattered to their cars—all except Fitzhugh, who no longer had a car.

"You son-of-a-bitch! Get him!" Fitzhugh broke into a run toward the passenger door of the nearest police car.

Fortunately for Lee Roy, he had thought of everything. Fitzhugh's hand flew off the door handle like he's been shocked. Lee Roy had greased the door handles and super-glued the locks on all the cruisers while the cops were busy with the road check. No one was going anywhere.

By the time they had called for backup on their handheld radios, Lee Roy Holder was long gone. The sheriff found Fitzhugh's car a mile down the road, unharmed except for the words "Lee Roy wuz here again" written across the windshield. It was parked at the entrance to a fire road. Tire tracks showed that Lee Roy apparently had left his four-wheeler waiting there, and escaped into the woods.

Fitzhugh insisted on a search party, but they finally gave up after a couple of days. Lee Roy knew those hills like the backside of the Women's Club president.

Captain Fitzhugh transferred out a week later, and Sheriff Charlie Stewart left the Most-Wanted List just like it was. I told him that Lee Roy wanted to remain the most-wanted man in Augusta County. Charlie decided it was safer for the sheriff's department to let him have his wish.

PART EIGHT

FORECAST CALLS FOR RAIN

May is a special time of year. There's Mother's Day, of course, but it's also the true beginning of summer. Augusta Countians can put away their jackets, and students can put away their books.

That's what makes it special for me. I'm not a student anymore, but every summer *The Wakefield Journal* gets a student intern. It's my chance to relax and let someone else do some of the work for a couple of months. That looked especially inviting with Georgia Burns in my life. I hadn't had a vacation since Bug Wake died and left me the newspaper. I was looking forward to a few uninterrupted days at the beach or a secluded chalet in the Smokies.

"I got another batch of intern applications, T.D.," Anabelle said, popping through my office door.

"Wow! How many does that make?"

"Batches or applications?"

"Applications."

"Three." She smirked when she handed me the latest.

Ordinarily, I was inclined to take applications from in-state college students—especially since those were usually the only college students who applied—but this year was different. The first two applicants were an agriculture major at the local community college and a literature major at the University of Alabama. Of the two, I would have preferred the ag major, but I was about to be spared from choosing between them.

The application Anabelle had just handed me was from an honest-to-God journalism major.

Rain Gullifer was from Maine and attended college in Connecticut. The letter didn't address how she heard of *The Wakefield Journal* in the first place, but everything was spelled right and it didn't mention Dante or Hampshire hogs. I picked up the phone and dialed.

⚜

"When do you think she'll show up?" Anabelle asked, interrupting me as I sorted press releases from the fax tray before leaving for the day.

"Who?" I scanned a press release, saw the phrase "extremely unique," and dropped it in the trash.

"Rain. You know, the hippie intern?"

"C'mon, Anabelle. You can't tell what she's like just by her name."

"Maybe not, but I bet her parents have tofu for Thanksgivin' dinner."

I chuckled in spite of myself. "You're probably right there, but you've got kids—you know how rebellious they are. She's probably a young Republican."

The bell over the door jingled and I turned to face the newcomer. She was about nineteen and skinny with a mass of tangled black hair pulled into two thick braids. She wore a black t-shirt and green army pants with tears all over them. A pair of tiny cat's-eye glasses sat on her nose, nearly hiding her eyes.

Anabelle gave me a "told-you-so" smirk and stood up from her desk.

"May I help you?"

"Yes, please. I'm Rain Gullifer. I'm supposed to start work here on Monday. Is Mr. Duff in?"

"I'm T.D. Duff," I said, sticking out my hand. Rain grasped it with a hand as delicate as a Champaign glass, but with the fingernails of a worm farmer.

"Did you find the place all right?"

"Yes. It wasn't difficult to find at all. I had some car trouble along the way, but I got it fixed up and everything's okay. I would have been earlier if not for that."

"Well, I'm sure you're anxious to get settled in and get all cleaned up and rested," Anabelle said pointedly.

"Yes, I am."

I was getting ready to leave anyway, so I put the press releases in Anabelle's inbox to be typed on Monday morning.

"My mother has a little apartment over her garage where you'll be living while you're here. You can follow me over and I'll show you where it is."

Rain followed me the three miles to Mama's house in her ratty green Volvo wagon. After showing her the apartment and helping her with her two backpacks, I left for Georgia's. Rain was supposed to meet us at the Red Bull Roadhouse in an hour, where I would treat her to dinner and get to know her before she started work on Monday morning.

Georgia and I got to the Bull early and left instructions for the hostess to bring Rain to the table when she arrived.

"So, T.D., I'm anxious to see what this intern looks like." Georgia's blue eyes twinkled as she said it. "How did you decide on her anyway? Did she send pictures with her application?"

"Of course. Nude pictures, actually. Why else would I hire her?"

"Why else?" Georgia agreed. She cast her eyes over my shoulder and spoke through her teeth. "Oh, my God, you would not believe what this girl looks like that just walked in."

"What?" I turned my head to look. Rain was walking self-consciously toward our table, her shoulders hunched and her face red. She still wore the same black t-shirt and the same green army pants she had on when I dropped her off, and her hair was still a mess. I stood up as she arrived at the table.

"Rain, come on and sit down. This is my friend Georgia. Georgia, this is Rain."

"Hello, Rain, nice to meet you."

"Is everything okay with the apartment? I know Mama had said there was some trouble with the plumbing, but I thought she got it fixed."

"No problems," she said.

The waitress was waiting for Rain to sit and handed her a menu. She pushed it aside.

"I'll have a salad."

"All right, honey. Will that be the chef salad, the crispy chicken salad, or the Famous Red Bull Sirloin Tip Salad?"

"Just a salad. Extra onion."

"What kind of meat do you want in it?"

"No meat. Just salad. Extra onion."

"Just salad?"

Rain looked put out. "I'm a vegan."

The waitress blushed, but looked at her with genuine pity.

"Don't worry about it, honey, you're still young. You'll find the right guy some day. You just gotta fix yourself up a little. And stop ordering extra onion."

Georgia kicked me in the ankle and smiled at Rain.

"So, Rain, that's a beautiful name. It makes me think of warm spring showers. What about you, T.D.?"

It was a strained evening. Rain seemed intelligent and articulate, but she wasn't much of a conversationalist. She finished her salad and looked at the steaks Georgia and I ordered with such disdain that we finally lost our appetites and the waitress picked up our plates. At the end of the evening, the only thing I had learned was that Rain could stare down a blind cat.

At least Rain was punctual. She got out of her car when I pulled up to the office thirty minutes before time to open on Monday morning. She had changed clothes and her hair was now brushed, but there was still a distinct smell of onions about her.

"Good morning, Mr. Duff."

"Hey, Rain. Are you ready to get started?"

"Yes, I'm ready, Mr. Duff."

"T.D.," I corrected, twisting the key in the door lock and letting her in. The press releases on the fax machine showed the county economic development director had called a news conference at 11:00 a.m., and I figured it would be a good chance for Rain to get her feet wet. Anabelle came in right behind us, so I gave Rain the assignment and left. It was supposed to be a beautiful spring day, and my favorite fishing hole was waiting. It was just as relaxing as I had hoped, and I was whistling a tune when I got back to the office at three o'clock.

"Hi, Rain. How'd it go?"

"Excuse me?"

"The meeting. How did it go?"

"Oh. Okay."

"What happened?"

"Just a lot of talking. I got some great pictures, though. They're hanging up in the darkroom."

I searched the darkroom over, but I couldn't find anything except some close-ups of rose buds.

"Rain? I can't find the pictures of the economic development meeting," I hollered through the open door.

Rain popped through the door and looked at me like I was crazy. She pulled down a rosebud photo and handed it over.

"It's a flower," I said. I'd never been afraid to point out the obvious.

"It's symbolism."

"Symbolism?"

"Something that evokes an idea or theme without boring people with a description."

"Yes, I know what symbolism is," I said, trying not to sound pissed off. "Why do I have a picture of a flower from the economic development press conference?"

"Because the guy talking said business is blooming."

"You mean 'booming?'"

"Oh. I'll go back and take a picture of the cannon at the war memorial."

"I've got a better idea. Why don't you write a story about what he said then make an appointment to go back and take a picture of something a little less symbolic? Like maybe the economic development director. Or the shell build-ing at the industrial site."

Rain wrinkled her nose in disgust.

"Okay."

A week later, the agriculture major and the literature major were begin-ning to look good to me. I sent Rain for a story about a fatal car crash and she came back with a picture of a soiled diaper on the roadside. I sent her for a story about a trial that had been moved from downstate to Augusta County, and I got a picture of the judge's ear. I assume she meant it to symbolize a hearing. On the other hand, Judge Randy Wilson did have the biggest, most unusual-looking ears of anyone I'd ever seen. I could save it for the fall when the local farmers started harvesting their cauliflower, but it was useless to me at the moment.

On top of the picture problems, there was no indication that Rain had yet discovered her apartment had a shower in it.

"I swear, T.D., if you don't tell that girl to take a shower, I'm going to hook up a water hose and ambush her," Anabelle complained.

"I know it's bad, but how do I tell a nineteen-year-old girl that she needs to shower?"

"Maybe if you wait long enough, you won't have to tell her. You think she'll figure it out when the plants by her desk start to wilt?"

"Anabelle!"

"Well, if the B.O. doesn't do it, the breath will. I swear, the girl must eat onion sandwiches. I have to step outside when she unpacks her lunch."

The bell over the door rang and Rain came through, sweat streaming down her dirt-streaked face. The breeze that followed her in wasn't fresh in the least.

"Hi! I've got some great pictures of the ducks on the river."

I held my breath the best I could.

"That's great. Why don't you go print them up?"

"Okay!"

Rain bounced off down the hall toward the darkroom, and Anabelle exhaled loudly.

"You've gotta talk to her, or you've gotta install windows that open."

"Maybe you could send her through a carwash," Georgia suggested. "Tell her you want the inside story on how one works."

"You're a big help. I wanted serious suggestions."

"I was being serious. Those big brushes would do wonders for her."

"You're a woman. Maybe you could talk to her."

"Oh, no. You're her boss. I'm just your cute, nice-smelling girlfriend," Georgia answered.

"Come on, I'm reaching here. Why should anybody have to tell her? Surely she knows. Three people have canceled interviews with her this week, and one of them was Danny Vaughn. He's worked with decomposed corpses and he can't even stand to smell her."

"You know, most people can't smell themselves. We become immune to our own aroma. Maybe you could trick her into showering."

"How could I do that?"

"Try taping a sardine can under her desk."

I gave up on Georgia's ridiculous suggestions. After two days, Anabelle threatened to quit if I didn't throw the sardine can away, and Rain apparently never realized it was there. I finally had a brainstorm of my own, and approached my friend Larry Stone for a solution.

"Larry, buddy, it's been a long time since you and Hilda had a pool party."

"You know, you're right. It's time, too. What do you say you and Georgia come over Saturday night? Hilda's going to Myrtle Beach with the kids, but I gotta work 'til Tuesday before I can leave. You can bring Georgia's roommate, too, by the way. Man, what tits."

I ignored the remark. "You mind if I invite some more people?"

"Sure, with Hilda gone we could have a hell of a party. Who'd you have in mind?"

"Oh, I don't know. Just some other people I know."

"How many?"

"One or two," I said vaguely. I took out my car keys and began searching for the ignition key.

Larry looked at me suspiciously. "Only one or two? Like who?"

"Anabelle?"

"That's one. Who's two?"

"Oh, just a friend from out of town."

"What friend?"

"A college friend."

"As in college intern???"

"Hey! There's an idea! Sure, I'll ask Rain to come. Thanks for thinking of her. You'll really make her feel welcome." I climbed in my Camaro and started the engine as I talked.

"T.D., that girl..."

"You're really a great guy, you know that? That's really cool of you to invite someone you've barely even met."

"T.D., she stinks!"

I raced the motor. "Man, you hear that ping? I think I better take this thing to Tolliver's and get it checked out."

"T.D., we just cleaned the pool!"

I already had the Camaro in gear and was backing out of Larry's driveway as he screamed the last remark at me. I had finally hit on a solution to the problem and I wasn't about to have my plan scuttled before it came to fruition.

I had two messages from Larry on my desk by the time I got back to the office, and three missed calls on my cell phone. Of course, I missed them intentionally, but I was beginning to feel guilty. If Larry really didn't want to host the swim party, I couldn't make him. On the other hand, if I didn't call back and try to talk him into it, he might just go to Myrtle Beach with Hilda and the kids, and lock the gate to the pool. I made a mental note to buy bolt cutters before the weekend.

Good ideas come in bunches, and I got my second one as I was scanning the note Anabelle had left from Larry. I grabbed the phone and called Georgia.

"Hi, hon, I've come up with a great idea to get You-Know-Who to take a bath, but I need a little help. Do you think you could get Joy to give Larry a call at the hospital?"

Joy Henderson was Georgia's roommate and fellow *Playboy* alumna. Since it was Larry's idea for her to come to the party, he would be falling all over himself to have it if she was sure to be there. Of course, his wife might not be happy with him when she found out, but I'd have to take that risk. Rain was going to go to that pool party, even it cost Larry a few nights in the doghouse.

Saturday was hot enough to peel paint, and I was never so happy with hot weather in my life. I had made all of the arrangements, including inviting Georgia, Joy, Anabelle and her boyfriend, Danny and Sherry, Kyle Pelphry, and, of course, the guest of honor. Anabelle, Danny, and Sherry all begged off when they found out Rain would be there. Kyle, being a game warden, had been sprayed by skunks more times than anyone else in Augusta County, so he figured Rain wouldn't be a problem. And, like Larry, he wasn't about to pass up a chance to see Georgia and Joy in swimsuits.

Hilda hadn't left for Myrtle Beach after all and answered the door. Surprisingly, she had a sympathetic smile on her face.

"Come in, come in," she said, ushering Georgia, Joy, and me into the living room. "Larry told me all about your little problem intern. I know exactly how you feel. I had a roommate in college who absolutely refused to take a shower for a month."

"Ouch. What did you do?" Georgia asked.

"Everyone on the dorm floor got together, and we firehosed her. Right there in her bunk. It helped her, but the carpet mildewed and it smelled almost as bad as she did."

"We'll try not to get your carpet wet," I said. "We're not going to hose her; we're just going to encourage her to take a swim, and we're all going to use the poolside shower before we get in. Maybe she'll get the hint."

An hour later, everyone but Rain had shown up. Larry, as always, had more beers than the rest of us combined and was being a bit too obvious looking at Joy in her swimsuit. She had taken the advice I had passed to her through Georgia and had worn a conservative one-piece, but there was only so much she could do to tone down her appearance. To her credit, Hilda had been a perfect lady to Joy. Larry wasn't so lucky.

"Larry, would you pass me the chips, please, sweetheart?"

"They're right in front of you."

"I can't reach them, honey."

Larry grabbed the chips absently and shoved them over. Hilda smiled sweetly and slipped her hand under the table.

"Thank you, honey bunch."

"Ow!" Larry's eyes bugged out even farther than they were already and he jumped out of his chair. "What the hell did you do that for?"

"Do what, dear?"

Hilda's face was pure innocence.

Larry blushed and rubbed the inside of his thigh.

"Nothing. I must have caught the hair on my leg in the chair."

He settled back into his chair and scooted it a little farther away from his wife. Joy smiled back at Hilda and pulled her cover-up on. "It's a little chilly out here, isn't it?"

"Damn straight it is," Larry grinned.

Hilda turned the ceiling fan off on the covered patio and scooted her chair closer to her husband. Larry got up hurriedly. "I think I'll go for a swim."

"You can't yet," I protested. "Rain isn't even here and we've got to get her into the pool. I can't take another week of her stinking up the office."

The sound of tires on gravel interrupted me and everyone around the patio shushed the person next to them. A moment later, the doorbell rang and Hilda went to answer it.

"What if she didn't bring a swimsuit?" Joy asked.

"It's a swim party—who wouldn't bring a suit?" I answered.

"We could all swim nekkid," Larry suggested, leering at Joy. "Ow! What did you do that for?"

Larry rubbed the rising welt on his arm and Georgia smiled as she put her flip-flop back on. "Hilda asked me to look after you while she was gone."

Hilda popped back through the door hurriedly, exhaling and then inhaling deeply as she hit the fresh air.

"Everybody, look who's here."

Rain trailed behind her, her oversized purse clutched to her chest.

A chorus of hellos went up from the patio. Larry got out of his chair and Georgia unobtrusively scooted over to give Rain a wide berth.

"Have a seat, Rain. Wanna beer?"

"No, thank you. But I would like to go for a swim. I go every day at home, but the public pool in Wakefield's too crowded. I haven't been swimming since I got here and I'm really anxious to get in the water."

"Well, we're anxious for you to get in, too," I stumbled. I could have kicked myself, but Georgia did it for me.

"Where can I change?"

Larry pointed her toward the cabana and she shuffled around the pool toward it.

"I told you this was a great idea," I said.

Georgia shrugged. "I had my doubts, but it looks like this might be really easy. I'll go ahead and start showering off, so she'll get the hint."

Georgia had just gotten into the water when Rain emerged from the cabana in a tiny black bikini.

Larry's jaw hit the ground and I'm sure mine did, too. Someone, maybe Kyle, made gagging noises.

"I haven't seen that much body hair since Hilda's mother wore a sun dress to the family reunion."

"You think she smells bad now...wait'll she gets out of the water," Kyle put in. "She'll be like a wet hound dog."

I still couldn't form words. Georgia stepped out of the poolside shower wiping water from her eyes. She stopped in her tracks as Rain walked briskly to the end of the diving board and jackknifed into the deep end. Georgia pinched the bridge of her nose, shook her head, and walked over to stand in front of me, her hands on her hips.

"You and your great ideas."

"But..."

"This is obviously going to take skills that you don't have. You just sit there and drink beer. I'll handle this. Joy, let's go."

The two spent the rest of the evening with Rain buttonholed between them in the pool, talking together like old friends.

Anabelle met me at the door Monday morning with a questioning look on her face.

"Well? Did it work? Tell me it worked. I can't take another day of holding my breath."

"Hold it a little longer and we'll see when she comes in. Georgia and Joy spent the evening talking to her, but I don't know what happened. Georgia wouldn't tell on the way home, and I haven't seen her since. I don't know what she's up to."

The next time the door opened, it wasn't Rain; it was Georgia and Joy—both dressed in conspicuously soiled clothes, their hair unwashed and smelling like a barnyard.

Anabelle recoiled in horror.

"Oh, my GAWD!"

"What happened to you two?" I asked, my eyes watering from the smell.

"We've been down to Lois Weber's farm, mucking out the horse stalls," Georgia replied, looking rather unhappy about the chore. "Then we helped slop the hogs."

"Why in the world would you do that?" Anabelle asked, cowering in the far corner of the reception room.

"We had a long talk with Rain Saturday night and we decided if you can't beat 'em, join 'em."

My heart sank. "Oh, no, don't tell me she's converted you."

"We haven't had a piece of meat or a slice of cheese since Saturday night," Joy confirmed. "And I'm ready to shoot Rain, Georgia, and myself. If this doesn't work, I don't know what we're going to do."

Georgia licked her teeth and made a face. "Have you ever had a peanut butter and onion sandwich? It's not good."

"I don't get it. What are you trying to do?" I asked.

"Well, since she apparently can't smell herself, we figured we'd give her a dose of our own scent. Maybe she'll realize how offensive she is."

Before I could think of a way to combat this logic, Rain's car swung into a parking place near the door.

"Here she comes. Let's hope it works quick."

The door of the now-familiar Volvo opened and a completely unfamiliar young woman stepped out. She was dressed in high heels, a knee-length business skirt, and open-collared cotton blouse. Her silky black hair hung nearly to her waist and it was the only hair in evidence. Not a single strand showed through the sheer stockings covering her shapely legs.

Georgia's mouth dropped open. "That's not..."

"I'm gonna kill her," Joy said.

The new Rain bounced through the door, her shoulders back and her head held high.

"Good morning, T.D., Anabelle. Georgia? Joy? What happened to you two? You really stink."

Joy's hands turned into claws and Georgia grabbed her before she could get them around Rain's throat.

"We were just helping a friend," Georgia answered. "Come on, Joy. Let's go get cleaned up."

Georgia shoved Joy out the door quickly and steered her toward the car.

"Man, they are <u>rank</u>," Rain chuckled.

"About that," I began. "I get the feeling we've been had."

Rain smiled a bit sheepishly. "Mr. Duff, I have a confession to make. I'm not really a journalism student."

"Oh, really?"

"You see, my professors gave you false references. I'm really working on my master's in psychology. My thesis is on Southern hospitality and societal norms. I was conducting an experiment to see how long it would take people here to be honest and tell me how bad I smelled, but you people are too nice."

Rain propped her elbows on the counter. "You guys never did anything to get me to clean up my act. You never even noticed, and I couldn't stand myself. I'm even having to leave my car windows down to let it air out."

"Well, we're just used to hog farms and hillbillies down here," I said.

The sarcasm was lost on Rain.

"Well, I'm sorry I punked you on the journalism thing. I wouldn't blame you if you fired me now."

"No, no. I understand completely. You know, it's a really pretty day for a walk. Could you, uh, take these obituaries over to the funeral home for me?"

"But I thought the funeral home sent those over here?"

"Well, no. We collect all the information and write them up and send them to the funeral home. Danny doesn't like dealing with the families."

"Oh. Okay." Rain took the stack of obituaries and walked off down the street.

"What did you tell her something like that for?" Anabelle asked. "I just took those off the fax machine to type."

"I'm writing a thesis on dumb Yankees."

"That's mean."

"I know," I said.

"Not mean enough, though. I'd fire her butt for lying in her application. And for making us smell her for the past few weeks."

"I thought about it, but I think she'll learn more about what she did wrong if she stays."

I waited until Rain's suddenly feminine figure had disappeared down the street, then I headed for the door.

"Call Danny for me, please, Anabelle. Ask him to play along and keep Rain there awhile. If she gets back before I do, try to think up some reason for her to leave again. Just make sure she leaves her car."

"Where are you going?" Anabelle called.

"Just down to the corner store," I assured her. "I suddenly have an over-whelming urge for tilapia."

PART NINE

HOMER AND THE
FLYING DOUGHNUT

I've always been an advocate of making people stand on their own two feet and making them learn from their own mistakes. That's why I never told Rain Gullifer about the fish I wedged into the springs under her car seat. I figure if she really wanted to get rid of the smell bad enough, she'd find it in the process of cleaning it.

Unfortunately, Rain's parents didn't share my view of discipline and self-reliance. Her dad, the hedge-fund manager, bought her a new Volvo before she left Augusta County, which was exactly a week after she revealed she had scammed me when she took her job as an intern, and proceeded to stink me out of the office with onion sandwiches and body odor. She protested that it was all in the name of science. Her study proved that Southerners can't deal psychologically with being rude.

I could have reasoned that the fish were placed in the name of science, too, but then I would have had to tell her I'd put them in the car, not to mention come up with some plausible scientific purpose for putting tilapia filets under a car seat in the festering heat of summer.

In the end, I took the easy way out and fired her. That also helped me with Georgia, who was still trying to get the odor of the pig farm out of her hair. I couldn't smell it, but she swore it was still there.

I was sleeping like a baby the night of the firing when the 9-1-1 pager on my bedside table started beeping. I normally turned it off, but I had forgotten that night. After knocking the alarm clock to the floor and answering a dial tone on the telephone, I finally woke up enough to associate the shrill tone with the correct electronic device.

I gave up chasing fire trucks and ambulances as soon as Bug Wake died and left the newspaper to me, but Sheriff Charlie Stewart had virtually forced the pager on me, apparently thinking such a show of openness and brother-hood would gain him some good coverage in the newspaper. Nothing much happened in Augusta County to warrant any coverage, good or bad, but a screeching pager in the middle of the night was still enough to pique my inter-est. A vague dispatch about a possible airplane crash scrolled across the green LCD screen, so I left the pager turned on for the rest of the night. The police had long-since gone to digital radios that were impossible to listen in on with a scanner, but if there really was an airplane crash, the dispatchers would page out a rescue squad sometime later in the night.

Unfortunately for me, but fortunately for pilots and passengers in the area, the pager stayed quiet and a phone call to the sheriff's department the next morning confirmed it was a false alarm. I was perfectly satisfied until 10:30 a.m.

That's when Homer Busch enlightened me.

A patch on the sleeve of Homer's wrinkled blue shirt announced that he was a guard for S.W.O.T. Security. At the moment, the tail of that shirt was hang-ing out and the buttons were undone, revealing a Skynyrd t-shirt underneath.

"T.D.! Huh, I gotta, huh, talk to you," Homer said as he huffed past Anabelle and straight into my office.

Homer had been the star running back at Augusta County High School when we were both sixteen, and he felt like he had earned the right to barge into my office and call me by my default first name. It must have been all those times he complained to the coach about giving me playing time, or the times he tried to stuff me in the trash can or pants me in P.E. that made him feel like we were friends.

But I wasn't one to hold a grudge—especially since time had done more to Homer than any revenge I could ever concoct. The former star running back would be lucky to run across the kitchen to the refrigerator now. He weighed at least three hundred pounds. His belly hung over the top of his uniform pants and out from under the bottom of his t-shirt, revealing angry red stretch marks on skin the color of wallpaper paste. His jowls quivered from the velocity of the air when he breathed.

I waited for him to launch into his story, but he was busy wheezing from the exertion of hustling into my office.

"I seen it, huh! I seen it!" Homer collapsed into my guest chair, testing the strength of its laminated legs.

"You saw what, Homer?"

"You ain't gonna, huh, believe it!"

"Well, if you already know I ain't gonna believe it, why the hell did you come down here?"

Homer shook his head emphatically, sat forward in his chair, and stabbed at my desk with one fat finger.

"'Cause I seen it! I don't give a damn whether you believe me or not, but you're the pitcher man and I want my pitcher in the paper."

I still didn't know what Homer had seen, and I wasn't sure how a picture of him in the paper would prove it. But if taking a picture of Homer would get his sweaty butt off my guest chair and out of my office, I was more than willing to get my camera out.

"Alright, Homer, I'll take your picture. Let's walk outside where the light's better."

"That's more like it," Homer said.

He stood up and took three steps toward the door before he stopped.

"Hey! You don't even know why you're takin' my pitcher!"

That's where Homer was wrong. I was taking his picture to get rid of him.

"Homer, you said it was worth putting your picture in the paper and I'm gonna put it in there."

"But ain't you gonna ask me what I seen?"

"I did. You said I wouldn't believe you."

"Well, you might believe me. Ask me again."

Sometimes it's hard not to roll your eyes when you're talking to somebody like Homer.

"Okay. Homer, what did you see?"

"A UFO. A visitor from another planet."

I was beginning to think Homer was from another planet.

"Aaahh. You saw a flying saucer?"

"When you say it that way, it sounds crazy," Homer snapped. "I didn't say a flying saucer; I said a UFO. It didn't look like a saucer at all. It was more like one of them long doughnut things they got down at the Sugar Shack."

"Chocolate or cream-filled?"

"I knew you wouldn't believe me."

"Well, Homer, you have to admit it's a little hard to swallow."

"Swallow this, Delaney: I got witnesses."

I gasped. My middle name had been a closely guarded secret forever, but Homer had just blurted it out as though everyone knew it. I jumped out of my chair and leaned across my desk.

"What did you say?!"

"I said I got witnesses."

"No, the other thing!"

"What other thing?"

"The part before 'I got witnesses.' Wait a minute…you've got witnesses?"

As it turns out, Homer had several witnesses. At least he said he had several witnesses. The story slowly unfolded, and the pager in the middle of the night and the lack of report by the sheriff's office began to make sense.

Homer was night-watching a strip mine a few miles outside of town when he saw the glow of lights behind a manmade knoll where workers were beginning to reclaim the site.

Probably some kids drinking beer and trying to get laid, Homer thought, but there were a couple of bulldozers over there that someone could vandalize. He turned off the portable television plugged into his cigarette lighter and started his pickup toward the light. He hadn't even made it to the road when the lights rose slowly into the sky and hovered just above the skyline.

"Let me tell you, I'm glad I had a cell phone. I called 9-1-1. I wasn't about to sit there by myself."

According to Homer, the UFO started to move slowly across the strip mine and he followed, using a C.B. radio and his cell phone to keep police apprised of where he and E.T. were until they arrived and took up the chase themselves.

"They followed it all over the top of that mountain 'til it finally started to move off over the valley. Some other cops picked it up there, and chased it clear acrosst Augusta County," Homer concluded.

"How do you know they chased it?" I asked.

"I heard 'em talkin' to each other on the radio."

"But you can't hear those radios on a scanner—they skip from channel to channel."

"I know that. Once the deputies got on the mountain, I got in the car with one of them."

Homer hadn't been wrapped too tightly since he lost his helmet in an away-game back in high school, but he sounded perfectly lucid if you left out the part about aliens and doughnut-shaped space ships. I had heard the page from the 9-I-I center, but that didn't prove anything. Any fool could pick up the phone and dial three digits, and all the pager proved is that this particular fool had.

"Homer, the pager didn't say a thing about a UFO. It said there was a possible plane crash."

"Do you think I'm a fool?"

I was beginning to wonder if he was psychic, too.

"I'm not going to call 9-I-I and report a UFO. If they sent anybody out at all, they'd send somebody with a butterfly net and a straight jacket. I told them I thought there was a plane going down."

Once again, Homer was making perfect sense. It was scary.

"So, uh, Homer, why didn't the deputies leave when they got to the job and you told them what you really saw?"

"I didn't have to tell them. They saw it themselves."

"Well, Homer, give me their names, let me take your picture, and I'll take it from there."

Ten minutes later, I had ushered Homer out the door.

"You surely aren't gonna put a picture of that crackpot in the paper and say he saw a UFO." Anabelle fixed me with her best disapproving look over the top of her glasses.

"Of course not. I'm going to put his picture in the paper and say he <u>said</u> he saw a UFO."

Sheriff Charlie Stewart was on the phone when I walked into his office. He smiled and waved me into a chair, rolled his eyes, and pointed at the receiver.

"Yes, ma'am. I'll be sure and keep my eye out for him. You take care now. Bye-bye."

Charlie hung up the phone and chuckled. "Lady says a pie is missing off her kitchen table, and she's sure Lee Roy Holder must'a slipped in and took it."

"People keep seeing ol' Lee Roy all over the county," I laughed. "He's like Elvis: everybody sees him at Burger King."

Lee Roy had made a career out of tweaking the police, and everyone seemed to see him except the cops. Charlie took it in stride, preferring to let Lee Roy be Lee Roy, as long as he tweaked the state police and left the sheriff's office alone.

"Next thing you know, they'll be seeing Big Foot," the sheriff said, laughing.

"Or UFOs," I added, laughing with him.

The smile froze on Charlie's face.

"T.D., I hate to rush you off, but I got a lot to do here today." Charlie stood up and started pulling on his jacket. "I gotta lead a funeral, and I've got car inspections to do. Good seein' you, though. You be good."

Charlie was starting out the door, but I was already up and walking that way, too.

"I'll walk you to your car."

"I, uh, I gotta go to the bathroom before I leave. No use in you waitin' on me."

Charlie ducked into the restroom and slammed the door. I sat on the corner of a desk and waited.

Five minutes passed before Charlie quietly opened the door and peeked around the edge of it. His face fell when he saw me still in the office, but he covered quickly and headed for the door. I went with him.

"Charlie, I already know your guys chased a UFO around the county last night. It's only gonna look worse if you don't talk to me about it."

Charlie frowned and kept walking. "You goin' crazy on me, T.D.? UFOs? When did *The Wakefield Journal* turn into a supermarket tabloid?"

"Ouch. That would sting if I was the sensitive type. Come on, Charlie, tell me what you know about this flying saucer...or flying doughnut or whatever the hell your guys chased."

"T.D., if you put something in the paper sayin' my deputies are out chasing UFOs, I'll be the laughing stock of the sheriff's association."

"So how's that any different?"

Charlie slammed his clipboard down on top of his cruiser.

"Now, dammit, that was one little mistake I made. They got no reason to keep laughin'."

"I know that and you know that, but the other sheriffs have a long memory."

Charlie pulled a cigarette pack from his pocket and shook a smoke out far enough to grab the filter with his lips.

"I thought you quit smoking."

Charlie pulled the cigarette out of his mouth, stuck it back in the pack, and tossed the pack in a trashcan on the sidewalk.

"T.D., if I tell you what B.S. this is, will you please drop it and not put anything in the paper?"

"I don't know, Charlie. I'll have to decide that after I hear the B.S. you tell me."

Charlie grabbed his clipboard and started back inside.

"Then I ain't sayin' nothin'. I'll call in the two doofuses that went on the call and you can talk to them. That way, if you do decide to print something, you can't quote me."

The two doofuses were deputies Gordon Long and Chris Patterson. Gordy had wedged his foot in the door of the sheriff's department by being a dispatcher and then a "special deputy"—an unpaid volunteer police officer who had driven his own ten-year-old Chevy, tricked out with blue lights and hand-painted sheriff's department markings until the sheriff finally hired him. He was a nice enough guy, but doofus was a charitable description.

Chris had followed a more direct route to being a fulltime deputy, but, like many other rural police officers, his sole training had been in the passenger seat of a patrol car while an older, also untrained, deputy drove around the county. Since the Augusta County Sheriff's Department didn't have the money to pay an officer for sitting in the passenger seat of a cruiser, Chris Patterson's training lasted all of four days while the sheriff had a radio and blue lights installed in Chris' surplus state police car.

Charlie had a dispatcher call them on the radio and asked that they meet me somewhere outside the sheriff's department. Not only did Charlie not want to talk about it, he didn't want to hear about it or even know about it.

I met Chris and Gordy at the mine site an hour and a half later, driving up the mountain on a gravel road packed hard and smooth as concrete by loaded coal trucks. The deputies were in Chris' dented gray cruiser, which was backed into a wide spot near the top of the entrance road. I swung my pickup in beside them and rolled down the window.

"Hey, guys. How's it goin'?"

Gordy spat tobacco juice into a foam coffee cup before speaking. "Goin' good, T.D. What can we do for ya today? Sheriff just said to meet you up here."

"He didn't tell you why?"

"Nary a word," Chris said. "What's up?"

"Well, I wanted to talk to y'all about the call you had up here last night."

"Oh! You mean the UFO?" Gordy asked as though it was the most natural thing in the world.

"Yyyyeah. That would be the call."

"Damnedest thing I ever seen," he declared.

Chris at least looked a little uncomfortable, but he still agreed with Gordy. "Sure was."

"Why don't you all show me where you saw...uh...it."

Chris looked at Gordy for an excuse, but Gordy was already bobbing his head in consent. "Fire 'er up and head up on the hill, Chris."

Chris started the Ford and pulled out of the wide spot, headed toward the strip mine. I got my truck turned and followed them. We only met two eighteen-wheel coal trucks on the way up the hill. A dozen more were lined up in a pit of coal to the right of the road we were on. Hundred-and-fifty-ton rock trucks moved from the adjacent area to a highwall in the distance to dump their loads.

We passed the active mine and drove a quarter of a mile along the flattened mountaintop along a road that wound through waist-high ceresa lespedeza and matted fescue grasses. We finally stopped at the edge of a knoll with a view of the vast, desolate plain, and Gordy and Chris got out of the cruiser.

"I thought Homer said he saw this thing on the active mine," I said as I got out of my truck.

"Well, he told us that's where it started, but by the time we got here, it had moved away over that holler-fill over yonder," Chris said, pointing to the west.

"So you saw a UFO?"

Chris looked uncomfortable again.

"Well, it was a flyin' object, and I couldn't identify it, so I guess you'd have to say it's an unidentified flyin' object."

"Well, what did it look like?"

Gordy and Chris looked at each other bewildered. Gordy scratched his buzz-cut head and spat tobacco juice.

"Well, it was kinda rectangular."

"It was longer than it was wide," Chris added.

That would be rectangular, I thought, but I decided to be a little more helpful than that.

"Homer said it was like a long doughnut."

I saw the light bulb go on over Gordy's head.

"Yeah! Like a longjohn!"

Chris, however, shook his head.

"A longjohn's too long and skinny. It was more like a bear claw."

"You're crazy…a bear claw's lopsided."

"Well, it wasn't like a longjohn. Or a twist neither."

"I never said it was a like a twist, but now that you mention it, the thing did have some uneven places on the sides like a twist."

"A twist is long and skinny, too. It was kinda more like a fritter—you know, all lumpy."

Following the exchange had been like watching a tennis match, but the John McEnroe and Bjorn Borg of doughnuts were just getting warmed up.

"It wasn't that lumpy. It was just a little lumpy. Like a beignet."

"You're right! A beignet! It was like a beignet with lights all around it," Chris confirmed, excited that they had finally nailed an accurate description of the pastry from another planet.

"Okay, so where did you see this beignet with lights?"

The two again pointed off to the west and launched into a story that was remarkably similar to the one Homer had already given me back at the newspaper office. The three of them had traveled from one edge of the mine to another following the elusive object, before driving off the hill and following it for many more miles until it finally disappeared over the mountains for good.

When they were finished, I snapped their picture with the strip mine as a backdrop and headed back to the office to figure out what exactly to do with a story about a UFO.

I figured it out just in time for the next edition. I reported it just as they told me, with pictures of Homer and of the two deputies. I resisted the urge to run an "artist's rendering" of a beignet with lights, but I couldn't resist having a little fun with the headline.

Homer's midnight odyssey
Deputies chase doughnut
across Augusta County

PART TEN

BIG FEET AND BIG NEWS

There is a short time of year between summer and fall when the sun still shines bright and hot, but the wind carries a hint of winter chill. The leaves are just beginning to change color, the grass is growing just a little slower, and the northern birds are beginning to pass through on their way to Colombia. School has started back, so there are no college students cruising through town booming hip-hop loud enough to shake the windows, and the teenagers aren't skateboarding down the sidewalk in front of the library.

All in all, it's a peaceful, but boring, time of year. The days seem to take weeks, and for some reason news slows down to trickle. This year, Georgia was gone out of town for a wedding, so I didn't even have her company.

The Wakefield City Council meeting was even more boring than usual this particular Tuesday evening. The councilmen approved the minutes of their last meeting, paid the city's bills, and adjourned without so much as a police chief's report. No arguments about ham or turkey for the employee Christmas bonus, since it wasn't close to Christmas; no questions about the mayor's expenses, since the mayor was on vacation and not available to needle; no complaints from citizens about the sewer smell on Water Street. Oakie Farlis, who was eighty-eight and had been a councilmember for more than forty years, didn't even pass gas. It was unheard of.

Since I was done in fifteen minutes, I decided to fight boredom at the 8-Ball bar.

I was enjoying my cold beer when Kyle came in, his game-warden uniform traded for a Corona t-shirt and a baseball cap. He ordered a beer and grabbed the bowl of peanuts off the bar as he headed over to my booth.

"Ev'nin', T.D."

"What's up?"

"Not a thing."

"Shit."

Kyle laughed as he scooted into the booth. "Ain't you heard? No news is good news."

"No news is no money for me. Not to mention the boredom. You know, Oakie didn't even fart at the council meeting tonight?"

"Can't be. Maybe you just couldn't tell."

"Yeah, like that's gonna happen. Don't you know of anything goin' on? Poachers? Somebody shoot himself squirrel hunting?"

Larry and Danny joined us before Kyle could answer. Larry sat three beers in front of him on the table, and I scooted over to let him in. Danny sat down next to Kyle and dropped a shot glass into his beer mug. "What's happenin', gentlemen?" Danny asked.

"That's what I was just asking Kyle. It's dead around here."

"In fact, it's not," Danny corrected. "I've been golfing every day this week. I haven't had a corpse since Thursday, and I only had one then."

"Did you have it for lunch or dinner?" Larry asked.

"Bite me, Larry," Danny said, taking a gulp of his boilermaker.

"Larry, how about you? Have you X-rayed any car wreck victims lately?"

Larry was finishing his second beer already and had to catch his breath before he could answer.

"Nope. Just run-of-the-mill lung disease."

"Damn. Kyle, you never did say if you had anything."

"Now that you mention it, I did run on a guy huntin' Big Foot."

I snorted and drained my beer, signaling for Frank the bartender to send another one.

"I'm not kiddin'."

"An honest-to-God Big Foot hunter?"

"Hand to God. He even gave me a business card."

"Big Foot hunters have business cards?" Danny asked.

"This one did. Said his name is—get this—Darwin, and he's a cryptozoologist."

"A crypto-what?" Danny asked.

"A crypozoologist," Larry said. "It's a person who studies animals that mainstream science discounts as hoaxes, myths, and hallucinations."

We all stared at him.

"Who are you and what have you done with Larry?" Danny asked.

"Hey, I read."

"Yeah, beer labels," Kyle snorted.

"Books," Larry replied. "And the Internet."

"Did these books have a lot of pictures?" Danny asked.

"Some," Larry admitted.

"Ah-hah!"

"But they had writing, too."

I turned back to Kyle. "So you think there might be a feature story in cyptozoology that wouldn't make people think they were reading headlines at the supermarket checkout?"

"What do you care? You wrote a story saying there was a UFO outside of town," Danny put in.

"No, I wrote a story saying three guys <u>claim</u> there was a UFO outside of town."

"My mistake."

"So, what do you think? Is the guy looney, or just mildly eccentric?"

"Except for believing in Big Foot, he seems perfectly sane. Said he's a college professor."

"Just because someone believes in Sasquatch doesn't make him crazy," Larry said defensively. "Sasquatch could very well be one of the last species of great ape on this continent."

"I guess that makes you the other one," Danny said, now finished with his drink and beginning to glow.

Larry raised the middle finger of his right hand at Danny and the index finger of his left hand at the bartender. "Gimme another beer, Frank."

He turned back to Danny. "They exist. I guarantee it."

I tried to ignore Danny and Larry. "Kyle, when you get home, call me with the information on that business card. If I interview him, it'll at least keep me from dying of boredom."

❧

Darwin B. Cooper, Ph.D., answered his phone when I called, and agreed to meet me at the entrance to Scotsman Branch Wildlife Management Area at noon the next day. When I arrived, he was sitting on the back bumper of his SUV, picking burrs off the legs of his canvas pants.

"Mr. Cooper?" I asked.

"Dr. Cooper, actually," he said, stretching out a hand to shake.

Much to my surprise, he didn't seem like a nut at all. Firm handshake, not too wide-eyed.

"Sorry. Dr. Cooper."

"Call me Darwin. People really get a kick out of my name, considering that I study primates."

"Primates? I thought you studied cryptids."

"Just particular kinds of cryptids—Sasquatch, Yeti—the primates. It's a sideline, really. I've done most of my research on great apes."

A few more questions and I learned that the good doctor was a professor of biology, and was taking a year's sabbatical to study cryptid primate stories in an attempt to determine whether there was any truth behind them. While he believed that it was possible such creatures existed, he had never seen one. He had seen unexplained tracks, and even played me a strange Tarzan-like yodeling he had recorded in the game preserve the night before, but he stopped short of saying it was Big Foot.

All in all, the interview was an island of interest in a sea of unending boredom and would make a nice little feature for *The Journal*.

I was in a much better mood by the time Georgia got back from her friend's wedding the next afternoon, and I was in a much, much better mood a couple hours after that.

We went to dinner at the Red Bull Roadhouse on Friday night and stopped by the 8-Ball afterward. When we walked in, Kyle was already there. He must have been watching the door because he sprang out of his chair and took a few quick steps toward us, waving in what I'm sure he thought was a furtive way.

"Hey, Kyle!" Georgia shouted.

"Shhh!" his finger flew to his lips and he glanced around quickly to see if anyone was looking.

"T.D.," Georgia muttered through a fake smile, "what is Kyle doing?"

I smiled back.

"I don't know, but I think he may be crazy."

We joined him at a booth in the back of the room, and he hunched over the table conspiratorially.

"You know that professor that was in here lookin;' for Big Foot?"

"Yeah."

"Well, he left last night, and he didn't find anything."

Georgia and I looked at each other. Then we looked at Kyle. Kyle looked back intensely.

"Wow, Kyle, I'm glad you told me that before deadline. I thought I wasn't going to have any news this week."

Kyle nodded knowingly. "Well, you do now."

I wasn't quite sure what to say. Kyle was usually the sanest person in Wakefield. Now I expected the next sentence to include something about a grassy knoll and a CIA conspiracy to kidnap Sasquatch.

"I'm not quite sure I'm following you here, buddy. He didn't find anything?"

"He didn't. But I did!" Kyle quickly shushed himself and blushed bright red. He looked quickly around the room to see if anyone was listening, but Tom Petty was playing too loud on the jukebox for anyone else to hear.

"You did what?"

Before he could answer, Larry bounced in the door and hollered out at us across the room. Danny sidled in behind him, his usual sunny undertaker's smile on display. Larry whistled for the bartender's attention and held up three fingers as he walked to the table.

"Hey, folks! What's shakin'?"

"Hey, Larry. Danny," I answered.

"Gentlemen, Georgia. Kyle," Danny cracked.

"You guys come on over," Georgia invited.

Kyle rolled his eyes and buried his mouth in his hand.

Larry caught the expression immediately.

"What's a matter, Kyle, don't want your ol' buddy Larry around?"

"We were just havin' a private conversation."

"Nobody I work with is gonna listen even if I tell them," Danny said.

Larry looked hurt. "So we're not included? I thought we were your friends, too."

Kyle sighed. "All right, I'll tell you. But you better damn well keep your mouth shut."

Danny nodded solemnly and Larry made a cross over his heart as the waitress placed a drink in front of Kyle. He kept his lips clamped in an exaggerated line until she left.

"Now, speak up. What's goin' on?"

Kyle's excitement had returned. He leaned over the table again and motioned us into the huddle.

"I found a Big Foot print."

"You shit," Danny said.

"I told you they were real!" Larry burst out, slamming his fist on the table. Kyle shushed him again. "Quiet!!"

"I told you they were real!" Larry repeated in a stage whisper.

"Oh, give me a break," I said. "Even the professor didn't really believe in Big Foot. He just found somebody who would pay for research."

"T.D., here you are with the game warden—a very credible witness—telling you he found Sasquatch prints, and you still don't believe it. You ought to be putting it in the newspaper. Why, it's practically a moral obligation," Larry said, poking his finger hard against the table for emphasis.

Kyle shook his head. "I don't want him to put it in the paper! Everybody will think I'm off my rocker."

"T.D., are you going to let a state official tell you what you can put in your newspaper and what you can't? It's a major scientific discovery!"

"I didn't say I found a Big Foot print; I said I thought I saw a Big Foot print."

"Don't change your story now—it just makes you look like you're covering something up. The government doesn't want us to know Sasquatch exists."

"The government doesn't even know about this! I haven't told anyone but you guys!"

"Well, what's holding you back? You should be shouting it from the rooftops. I think you should tell everybody what you saw. Call the professor back. Give T.D. an interview. Call CNN!"

"Wait, slow down! I'll call the professor back, but I'm going to wait to see what he says before I tell anybody else."

Danny cleared his throat. "Well, Kyle, you've been a game warden long enough that if you tell me you saw a Sasquatch footprint, I believe you. I don't need the professor to confirm it."

"Don't listen to him. What are you waiting for?" Larry asked. "Go call him."

"I didn't say he should call; I just said I don't need some professor to tell me. I believe Kyle. I still think you should call him, though," Danny said.

"Damn straight he should call him. You are gonna call him, ain't you?" Larry prodded.

"All right, I will."

"Go on."

"I'm goin'."

"Chicken."

"Am not!"

"Are so."

"I am not!"

"Then call him."

"I will." Kyle put a ten-dollar bill on the table for his beers, and pushed Larry out of his way so he could get up.

"Put a twenty on it?"

"On what?"

"Twenty says you won't call."

"I'd love to take your money. You're on."

Kyle stormed out of the bar and Larry sat back down, grinning.

"T.D., you gotta put it in the paper."

"Larry, I am not gonna put anything about this in the paper. But I will help you make more tracks—if you tell me how you two did it."

Larry's mouth dropped open. "How did you...?

"It's Friday night, you're still relatively sober, and you're not wearing scrubs, which means you didn't work today. In fact, you're wearing brand-new camouflage, and I know for a fact you haven't had a hunting license since you got drunk and fell out of your tree stand. You sold me your rifle, remember? On top of that, Danny still doesn't have any names on the board out front of the funeral home and there's a pine twig stuck in his collar. I'd expect that if he had been golfing, but he hasn't because he's not wearing his lucky golf shirt."

I have to admit I was pleased by the open mouths on the other side of the table.

"Damn, you're good," Danny said. "Why are you still in Wakefield?"

"I ask myself that question at least once a week. Are you gonna show me what you did?"

"Meet me at my place at five in the morning."

I rarely see 5:00 a.m., but curiosity is better than any alarm clock. I was at Larry's house at quarter to five, and the Suburban from Danny's funeral home was already in the driveway. The light was on in the garage, so I went in through the side door without knocking. Danny and Larry were sitting on barstools by the work bench, drinking coffee.

"Good morning!" Danny hollered, raising his coffee mug in a toast. Larry winced at the volume of the greeting, but nodded, too.

"Morning. What's a matter with you, Larry?"

"My head's killing me."

"You? Hungover? I don't believe it."

"I must not have drunk enough last night. This usually doesn't happen to me."

He climbed off the stool, dragged a large plastic tote over in front of me, and took the lid off.

"You wanted to know how we made the tracks? Here you go."

I looked down into the tangle of square metal tubing and cables.

"What is it?"

Larry grinned proudly in spite of his headache, and pulled on a piece of tubing. He took out a stilt with a large rubber foot attached to the bottom and set it on the bench.

"This is Harry," he said.

"Harry. Original."

"Not really," Danny said, missing the sarcasm. "Remember that old T.V. show about the family that ran over a Big Foot and took him home to recuperate? They named him Harry, so we thought we would, too"

"No kidding." Danny finally got it and frowned.

"Well, don't ask if you don't really mean it."

"Sorry. Again, what is this?"

"This," Larry said, "is the ultimate robotic Sasquatch foot. Well, not really robotic; it's more like a puppet."

"Well, at least it's not the only dummy in here," I said.

"Now, I know Larry sounds a little crazy right now, but this thing really does make a hell of a convincing footprint," Danny said.

"A lot of people have been convinced by footprints made with a hunk of plywood."

"Nobody that matters," Larry sniffed. "But this one could fool experts. It ain't just a 'hunk of plywood.'"

"I can see that, but I don't think you're going to fool an expert with a hunk of rubber, either."

"Wanna bet? All of these other footprints people have made have been simple—just a flat, foot-shaped hunk of plywood or ceramic. This one is different. It takes into account all of the things that experts look for. I built a skeleton foot out of metal rods then covered it in layers of cables wrapped in rubber muscles, just like a real foot." Larry was talking faster and faster. "It's articulated. Every step I take with this, the foot interacts with the substrate. The width of the toe pads and spacing between the toes varies with the type of surface."

I know my mouth was hanging open after the first two sentences, but I couldn't muster the effort to close it. I shook my head to clear it.

"Do I know you?" I asked.

"I think Larry's been kidnapped by aliens out of that UFO you had in the paper," Danny said.

Larry gave him the finger.

"I'm telling you, I've studied this. I can fool anybody."

I thought a minute, calling up all of the detective novels I'd read and all the television police shows I'd ever watched.

"No, you couldn't. A real foot has fingerprints. I mean toe prints, or something."

"Dermal ridges," Larry corrected with a smirk. "It was a bitch, but I took care of that, too. Humans have horizontal ridges. Apes have diagonal ridges. Harry," he picked up the steel and rubber foot and waved it in front of my face, "has longitudinal dermal ridges."

"Scary, huh?" Danny said.

"Scary is right. If Larry can do this, Big Foot may really be real."

We tromped through the woods for a quarter of a mile with rugs strapped to our feet before Larry replaced his rugs with the Harry stilts in a patch of rocks high up on a hill and headed off through the woods. Danny pulled a couple of beers out of his fanny pack and handed one to me.

"You gotta admit, T.D., this is one hell of a practical joke."

"I'm not sure 'joke' is the right word, but it is one hell of a whatever-it-is."

I popped the top on my beer and took a drink. "How long does he do this?"

Danny considered the question as he unfolded the legs on a high-powered spotting scope and peered through the eyepiece.

"Not long. As perfect as he says this is, he's afraid if he makes too many tracks, he'll get caught."

Danny chuckled as he gazed out over the forest. "He may get caught sooner than he thought. Kyle's coming up the other end of the path, and he's got somebody with him."

I took the end of the scope from him and focused on a clearing atop a knoll a half-mile away. "Crap. That's Dr. Cooper."

"The Big Foot expert? That's hilarious! Larry'll run right into him with his stilts on."

"This is serious. I don't think the professor will think this is funny. Call Larry's cell phone and warn him."

"I'm not calling his cell phone. He's got that stupid Frogger ring on it. You can hear it a mile away."

"Well, how are we gonna warn him?"

Danny thought for a minute then took a deep breath and let out a loud, warbling yell.

"What the hell! Kyle can hear 'Frogger,' but he can't hear that?"

"It's a Big Foot call. I've heard Larry do it a dozen times. If they hear it, they'll be looking for a Sasquatch."

"No, they'll be looking for George of the Jungle."

Danny took another deep breath and yodeled again.

I looked through the scope and saw Larry running toward Kyle and the professor as fast as the ungainly Big Foot stilts would let him, crashing through brush and breaking tree branches as he went. Kyle and the professor were running toward the car, breaking even more branches.

"He's running straight toward them!"

Danny grabbed the scope and chuckled. "He's not running toward them; he's running away from us!"

I pushed Danny away from the eyepiece again. Larry was running through the clearing and looking back over this shoulder, a look of pure panic on his face. He turned his head forward just in time to get one stilt hung up in the underbrush, sending him sprawling into the forest.

"What's happening?" Danny asked.

"Larry just fell face-first into a briar patch."

Danny laughed. "That's classic. I gotta call him. Kyle's gotta be gone by now."

He pulled out a cell phone, put it on speaker, and dialed Larry's number. I watched as Larry struggled to his feet and groped in his pocket as he ran.

"What!?" he screamed into the phone.

"Larry, man, what's goin' on? Where are you?"

"I'm in the friggin' woods. Where do you think I am?"

"We lost sight of you. Why are you runnin'?"

"Didn't you hear that scream? That's exactly like the one they had on the Internet. It's a real Sasquatch and he's right behind me!"

Danny shoved his fist in his mouth to stifle a laugh.

"Man, are you sure? We heard something, but we thought it was you trying to scare Kyle," I said.

"It wasn't me."

"Well, slow down, man. I saw Kyle running through the woods ahead of you."

"Slow down nothing! I'm getting out of here. Pick me up at the parking lot on the other end."

Danny was on the ground laughing. I shielded the mouthpiece to keep Larry from hearing.

"All right, man. If you're that sure it's a Big Foot, we're gettin' out of here, too."

The ride home was difficult. It was almost impossible for Danny to contain his laughter and it wasn't much easier for me. Thankfully, Larry had no trouble believing that we were laughing at the way he crashed through the bushes, never thinking for a moment that there might be more to the joke than just his pratfalls.

It was funny until the next day.

"T.D.! You'll never guess who's coming!" Larry shouted as he hurried across the 8-Ball toward the table where Danny and I were sitting.

I took a sip of beer and swallowed slowly while I considered the challenge.

"Let me see...the British?"

"No, smartass. Zorro!"

"Is he bringing his sword?"

"Not that Zorro, dummy."

I frowned at him. "You mean there's another Zorro?"

"Relámpago."

"Relámpago?" I turned the word over in my head and a faint alarm bell began to ring in the back of my memory. "Zorro Rel...? Zorro Relámpago???"

The tabloid T.V. reporter/anchor of a major cable network was the last name I had expected, and the last one I wanted to hear as well.

"He heard about the Sasquatch, and he's coming to do a report!"

I choked on my beer, and Danny beat on my back while I coughed convulsively.

"Well, don't get all upset about it. I tried to get you to write a story, but noooooo. You wouldn't have anything to do with it."

"So you called Zorro??"

"Of course not. I mean, I may be pissed at you for not doing a story, but you're still my bud. I wouldn't do that to you."

"I'm glad to hear..."

"He called me after I filled out the news-tip form on his web site."

Danny laid his head on the table and shook with laughter.

"What's he cryin' about?" Larry asked.

Danny was in the embalming room when I got to the funeral home the next morning, but his assistant, Milton Lee, was sitting at a desk in the office reading a magazine.

"Hey, Milt, it's pretty important for me to talk to Danny. Do you think he would mind if he was interrupted?"

"Prob'ly not. You can just go on down."

"To the embalming room? Uh, no. I meant could you interrupt him?"

"That wouldn't be a good idea."

"You mean he wouldn't mind if I walked in on an embalming, but he'd be mad if you did?"

"No, he wouldn't mind."

"But you just said it wouldn't be a good idea. I thought you meant Danny would get mad."

"No, but you see, I've got a bad back and if I interrupt him, he'll want me to take over."

"You think you could risk it?"

Milton frowned at me but opened the door at the top of the stairs and yelled down.

"Danny! T.D. wants to see you!"

Danny's voice wafted up from the basement. "All right. Can you come down and finish this up?"

Milton frowned at me again and trudged down the stairs. Danny came up a minute later, muttering under his breath.

He slammed the door and went to a sink beside the basement door.

"Danny, we gotta do something. We can't let that half-baked T.V. showboat come in here and make us all look like jackasses."

"Oh, relax. Zorro rarely makes anybody look like a bigger jackass than he is."

"Danny, that's pretty big."

"Good point. You think we can discourage him from coming?"

"I doubt it. He's supposed to be here this Thursday afternoon, and he's staying for three days."

"What do you wanna do?"

"I've been thinking about that. I want him to go live," I said.

"What do you mean live?"

"I mean an hour-long special—no tape, no safety net. Just like Geraldo and Al Capone's vault."

"That just ended up making Geraldo look like a fool."

"Exactly. Let Milton take care of your downstairs client and come with me. We've got a lot of work to do."

Larry wasn't happy when he found out the Big Foot he ran from only wore size twelve loafers, but after he got over his initial anger, he began to see things from my point of view. Nobody wanted to be the target of a T.V. "news" story that ended with the words, "Beware the mark of Zorro." He called Zorro on his cell phone and began the process of pitching a live show, while Danny and I called on Kyle to suggest a remedy to the Big Foot problem. And as badly as I hated to do it to Kyle, the suggestion did not include the revelation that Danny had made the Sasquatch howl that sent him and the professor running back to the parking lot.

Zorro never called back, so we were on pins and needles until Thursday afternoon when a white box van with a seven-foot-tall toothy picture of Zorro's head on the side and a satellite dish on the top pulled up in front of *The Journal* office. Behind it was a one of the biggest, most ostentatious motor homes I had ever seen, and when the door opened, the biggest, most ostentatious jackass I had ever seen stepped out.

I stared over my glasses as Zorro pulled a compact from his pocket and checked his hair. Anabelle gaped in horror.

"A compact?? The man carries a compact?"

"Yeah. Uh, Anabelle, I'm not really in the mood to talk to this guy. Could you take care of these news releases? I'm going out the back way."

I left the stack of releases I had been reading on the counter and ducked down the hallway as Zorro's videographer pulled his camera out of the truck.

Two days of careful preparation later, Zorro's live show, *The Search for Sasquatch*, was being endlessly advertised on his network. Larry had been interviewed, the professor had been interviewed, and I, thankfully, had not. As the time for the show approached, Danny and I pulled a rented R.V. into the campground just down the road from Scotsman Branch Wildlife Management Area. A quick adjustment of the satellite dish on the roof, and we were watching cable news.

"Two minutes and counting," Danny observed, setting three beers out on the table. "Want some popcorn?"

"Yeah, sounds great," I said, popping the top on my PBR.

A second later, Larry yanked the door open and jumped inside. "All set. I told him there was no way in hell I was going back into those woods this late in the evening."

"Well, you'll look like a coward on international television, but maybe people will forget about it by the end of the show," Danny said, punctuating his opinion with a burp.

"If Zorro can follow directions, they'll forget about it," Larry assured him.

The microwave beeped and Danny opened the popcorn bag and poured its contents into a bowl. The ultra-modern Spanish-inspired theme music came on television and a large letter "Z" slashed across the screen, a blatant rip off of the 1960s T.V. series.

"Good evening, I'm Zorro Relámpago."

Taped video of Wakefield flicked past then the camera returned to Zorro, his blue-black hair greased back, his beard perfectly clipped into a rugged, three-day growth of stubble. "The tiny town of Wakefield. It's a quaint village nestled in a 'holler' of the Appalachian Mountains. But this village is stalked by a monster.

"Tonight, I stalk the monster—alone. My guide, Wakefield native Larry Stone, was too fearful of these woods to enter them at night. He brought me here then high-tailed it back to the safety of town. I'm here alone, except for my cameraman, and somewhere in these woods," he paused and gave the camera a courageous glare, "Big Foot."

The show plodded along for awhile, interspersing commentary from Zorro with taped interviews. T.V.-news-Larry, dressed in a flannel shirt buttoned to the collar and a Tractor Supply hat, sat in front of the sign to the wildlife management area.

"Dang! You look like you're waiting for your brother Darrell and your other brother Darrell," Danny cracked.

"Shh, I'm talkin'," Larry said.

"He made the awfullest scream you've ever heard. It echoed off the hills 'til you couldn't tell which direction it was coming from," T.V. Larry said.

"As you can see, here in these hills, the uneducated, superstitious locals are so scared of the Sasquatch that they can't even think of chasing it," Zorro said, shaking his head sadly.

Larry slammed his popcorn bowl down on the table, sending fluffy white kernels flying out onto the floor. "Uneducated??? Why, that pompous horse's ass! I've got a bachelor's degree in radiological technology. I oughta go across the road and smack the living shit outta that...that..."

I patted him on the shoulder and took the bowl he had thrown down. "Easy there, big fella." I stuffed the last handful of popcorn in my mouth and handed the empty bowl back to Larry.

The show continued in much the same vein, but now Zorro was tiptoeing through the woods, branches snapping and leaves rustling.

"I am now in the area that my research tells me is near-perfect for Big Foot activity," Zorro whispered loudly into his microphone.

"That's where I took him to today," Larry explained.

"How did he find it again in the dark?" I asked.

"I tacked CDs to the tree trunks so he could find his way."

On television, Zorro was stooped over, pointing to something and waving for his cameraman to come closer.

"Just as I suspected. I have discovered a Sasquatch track on the trail. It's a huge footprint. This one's a big boy."

Larry chuckled. "I wonder if he could've found it if I hadn't showed it to him today."

Zorro launched into an explanation of catching a Big Foot, telling the television audience about the strange cry a Sasquatch makes and how a successful hunter can call one to him by making such a call.

We burst out laughing and Danny got up quickly to open the door of the R.V. I turned the volume down, and we all ran out the door and listened. We could hear the faint warbling cry from the woods. A moment later, we heard a similar cry a little farther off. We fell over each other getting back to the television. Zorro was excitedly moving toward the sound of the other call. He stopped and yodeled then charged ahead when he heard the other call again.

Ahead, the night-vision camera picked up a dark opening in the bushes, and Zorro turned toward the lens.

"Just as my source...research shows, the sound appears to be coming from this cave," Zorro whispered. "I'm turning on my mini-cam now."

The screen split as Zorro put on a headband with a tiny fiber-optic camera lens mounted on it. The section on the right side of the screen showed the view from that camera as Zorro got down on his knees and began crawling into the hole.

"You gotta hand it to him," Danny said. "He's got balls."

"But no brains," Larry smirked.

I shushed them both and scooted closer to the television.

"I'm inside the cave now. Keep in mind that what you're seeing is on a night-vision camera. I am in total darkness now. There seems to be something blocking my path now. Hold on."

There was a fumbling noise and a bright light flared on the right of the split screen as Zorro turned on his flashlight. There was lesser flare on the left and it became clear that the "cave" was perfectly round. The cameraman tried to get Zorro's attention, but the star wasn't listening.

"This is odd. It looks like steel."

The camera showed Zorro's hand rise and stretch out to the steel bar. He tugged hard and a there was a loud clang as the camera on the left showed a steel gate fall. A half-dozen Fish and Wildlife employees jumped out of the bushes and surrounded the "cave."

"We got it! We got it!" Spotlights came on, blotting out the view of the trap on the night-vision camera outside.

"Hey, who are you? What are you doing here?"

On the right side of the screen, the camera shook convulsively as Zorro turned around and looked out through the bars.

"Cut the camera! Cut! Turn it off!"

A moment later the screen went blank and the picture changed to a befuddled anchorman at a desk in New York.

"Ladies and gentlemen, we are experiencing some technical difficulties and we've temporarily lost contact with Zorro Relámpago. As soon as our connection is renewed, we'll take you back to the woods of Augusta County. We'll be right back after this break, and hopefully soon we'll have an analyst who is familiar with that part of the country to talk about what may be going on there."

Fortunately for me, *The Wakefield Journal* didn't need an analyst to know what was going on.

As soon as Danny, Larry, and I were able to pick ourselves up out of the floor, we turned the R.V. back toward town and *The Journal* office, so I could compose the headline for the story I already had written.

Bear trap leaves mark on Zorro

PART ELEVEN

SHELTER ME

Anabelle stopped filing and rushed to the counter when the bell jangled over the front door of *The Wakefield Journal*.

"Well?"

"Well?" I asked.

"Well, what happened? Was anybody killed?"

"One."

Anabelle shook her head sadly. "Who was it?"

"Not sure. He didn't have any identification on him."

"Now, T.D., you know everybody in the county. Didn't you get a look at his face?"

"Yeah, but it was lying in the middle of the highway. I couldn't really tell who it belonged to."

Anabelle turned pale. "Ewww! In the middle of the highway? Did it decapitate him?"

"Naw, just peeled his face off. A coil of steel fell off the back of a flatbed. That stuff's just like a meat slicer. Speaking of which, I'm starving. I gotta go pick up Georgia and get a sandwich. You hungry?"

"Not anymore," Anabelle said dryly. "How can you eat after that?"

"If it was a person, I'd probably have a harder time, but a sliced-up deer doesn't bother me much. If it did, you'd never get any more of my venison chili." I smirked as Anabelle leaned forward and thumped her forehead on the counter.

"A deer. The victim was a deer." She straightened up and threw a pencil at me. "Get out of here, T.D., before I throw you out in traffic."

I laughed as I put my camera in my office and grabbed the phone to call Georgia. I was late for lunch, but she had waited for me.

"Pick me up in five. I'm starving," she ordered.

"I'll be there."

Fall can be fickle in Augusta County. Just yesterday, the temperature never got out of the sixties, but today the mercury was hovering around eighty-two. Car wrecks are bad anytime, but on a hot day, the sight of remains—even deer remains— cooking on the asphalt and the smell of blood can really put you off your feed. I shook the images out of my head. Anabelle had planted the seed in my mind, and if I wasn't careful, eating was going to be out of the question. And I really wanted lunch.

There wasn't a breath of air stirring when I went out to the car, and the drive to Georgia's office would have been unbearable without the air conditioning. A gray haze muted the blue sky.

By the time I reached the office of Van Hoose, Van Hoose, and Vanderpool, the gray haze had turned into a threatening gray wall just over the western horizon.

"Hi, hon," I said, leaning over to smooch Georgia as she hopped in the passenger side of my Impala.

"Don't mention honey. I'm starving," she said. "Where have you been?"

"Oh, working on a story."

"Well, let's go work on a steak. The Red Bull shouldn't be crowded this late."

I dutifully drove to the Bull and got us a table near the back.

Georgia ordered the "A lot of bull" special, a sixteen-ounce Angus ribeye with a loaded baked potato, and two plates of vegetables and chicken wings from the hot bar. That was after her salad and before her dessert plate.

I couldn't help but stare.

Georgia looked up at me suspiciously, her mouth full of broccoli casserole. "Mfaht?"

"Nothing."

"Mfahtta ya mean, nuffing?" she asked around the casserole.

"I just can't figure out how somebody built like you can eat like that."

She blushed and swallowed.

"I'll work out when I get home."

"Okay."

When Georgia finally finished and I paid the check, we walked out into an oppressive atmosphere.

The dark ridge of clouds along the horizon now filled the sky, and a brisk wind was blowing in from the south. Georgia grabbed my arm as the wind caused her to lose her balance. We held on to each other as we ran to the car and shut the doors against the weather.

"T.D., I don't like this," Georgia said, leaning forward to look up through the top of the windshield. "It reminds me of when I was a little girl in Georgia. It's tornado weather."

I flipped on the radio and backed out of the parking place as the first drops of rain splattered on the windshield.

We were pulling to the highway when the emergency alert buzzer cut into the middle of Lynyrd Skynyrd's "The Breeze," and an automated voice replaced Ronnie Van Zant's.

"The National Weather Service has issued a tornado warning for the following counties: Allen, Augusta, Barber, Buchanan, Calhoun, Harlan, Lee, Roane, Wise. At three-fifteen, a funnel cloud was spotted five miles southwest of Wakefield. The storm was moving north at sixty-five miles per hour..."

I punched the time button on the radio and the digital display changed to 3:17.

"Crap! We've gotta get to a shelter."

"There's one in the basement of the Presbyterian church," Georgia said.

I gunned the car and drove two blocks to Willet's Memorial Presbyterian, parking crossways of the yellow lines in the parking lot. Georgia and I ran through drenching rain and in the side door of the basement.

We followed signs taped to the wall to a solid plank door at the end of the basement that was buried in the hillside. Three others were already inside and a weather radio blared out the latest news.

"Hey, T.D.!" Jason McQuaid hollered as we shoved open the door and hurried inside.

Jason was Augusta County's newest—and only—OB/GYN doctor. I had known him since elementary school, and couldn't bring myself to call him "Doctor." Given his propensity for flirting, the fact that he had become a gynecologist/obstetrician was a running joke around the county. For that matter, the fact that he had become a doctor of any kind was a running joke.

Hard work was something he had never been known for, and while he was obviously highly intelligent, he never seemed to care much for applying his mental abilities. He had a penchant for golf, pretty women, and hard liquor, and had apparently been involved in at least two of those pursuits before the storm hit.

He was dressed in a green Izod shirt, blue slacks, and golf cleats, his curly brown hair peeking out from under a porkpie hat, and his face was covered in a two-day stubble. He belched loudly and wobbled in his chair.

Melinda Creech rolled her eyes and turned around in her chair, putting her back to the doctor. Like Jason, she had been a schoolmate of mine, though I rarely saw her anymore. Known as one of the horniest girls in high school, she married at seventeen and promptly began popping out babies like a Pez dispenser. She always brought their pictures in to be put in the paper when they were born, had birthdays, or got an award at school, but I had lost count of how many she actually had. Given the frequency of her visits to the office, I was sure the number was somewhere between fifteen and twenty-three.

She shifted around and tried to cross her legs, but her pregnant belly prevented it. Instead, she spraddled her legs out, propped her elbow on the back of her chair, and looked miserable as she greeted us.

The third occupant was a newcomer to Wakefield. I was sure of it because in a town as small as Wakefield, I would have remembered her. She was almost—I said "almost"—as gorgeous as Georgia, but she was dressed rather severely in a mid-calf-length khaki skirt and striped, button-down shirt. Her honey-blond hair was pulled up in a bun. She smiled when we came in and stuck out her hand.

"I'm so glad you two came in here out of the storm. I'm Cindy Nelson. My husband is the new minister here," she said, pumping first Georgia's hand then mine.

Georgia gave her our names, and made the obligatory niceties, and then Cindy scurried off to find refreshments. She gave Jason a wide birth. He gave her a wide leer.

The storm was getting even stronger outside and I had to yell to be heard even in the enclosed basement.

"Finish your game before the storm, Jason?" I asked, nodding at his clothes.

"What game?"

"Golf?"

"Oh! I just went to the bar. I never got around to teeing off."

Georgia shut her eyes and shook her head slightly in disgust. I grabbed a chair from one of the tables and turned it backward to sit.

"Melinda, how are you doing?"

"I'm bloated."

"Ah. I see. I mean, I don't see. You don't look bloated at all," I said, trying not to look at her puffy lips or her swollen ankles.

"Don't try to be nice. I look like I should be tethered to a float at the Macy's Thanksgiving Day Parade."

"Well, it won't be much longer, will it, Doc?" I asked, trying to get out of the conversation.

"How the hell should I know? I'm not her doctor."

"Oh? I thought you were the only OB/GYN in the county."

"I wouldn't go to him if he was the only gynecologist in the country. I wouldn't let him look at it for free in high school; I damn sure ain't payin' him to look at it now," Melinda said sourly.

"Like I wanna see it anyway," the doctor snapped.

"OB, my ass! SOB," Melinda countered.

"Cookies, anyone?" Cindy asked, shoving the plate in front of Jason.

"Thanks, cupcake," he said, taking one.

Melinda grabbed a half-dozen, leaving one each for Georgia and me. I politely declined, and Georgia took both of them.

The storm was howling outside, and Cindy had turned the weather radio to alert mode to cut out some of the noise. It would sound an alarm if another warning were issued. Personally, I wished she'd left it on to drown out the noise from Jason and Melinda.

Georgia and I retreated to a far corner of the room, and Melinda and Jason finally stopped sniping and turned their backs to one another. The pastor's wife flitted uncomfortably about the room doing meaningless chores and stealing worried glances at Jason and Melinda.

The storm was still crashing outside when the shrill screech of the weather alarm sounded again. We waited for an announcement, but it never came. I suddenly realized that the screech wasn't the alarm—it was Melinda.

She was sitting bolt upright in her chair puffing like a steam engine, both hands clutching her belly. A puddle was spreading under her chair.

"Well, hell. It looks like I'm going to have to do this after all," Jason said, rolling up his sleeves.

"Like hell you are," Melinda answered between puffs. "There are four other people in this room."

Jason scoffed. "You can't even count. Cindy, T.D., and Georgia make three."

"And I make four. I've got six kids—you think I don't know how to deliver this baby myself?"

"Now, Melinda, think this over. There's a doctor right here in the room. You know you can't do this by yourself," Georgia urged. "Besides, you know how clumsy I am. I'd be afraid I'd drop it."

Melinda's mind clicked behind the pain-clouded eyes. She was no doubt remembering the time Georgia dropped her bowling ball and sent a guy two lanes away to the emergency room.

"All right, then there's two other people in the room," she said.

Cindy was standing flattened against the wall, her face white as a sheet.

"I get sick at the sight of chicken blood," she said.

"EEEEYYYYYYYYYYYY!!!!!" Melinda let out another screech and Cindy sprinted through the door to the kitchen.

"T.D.! Get over here," Melinda ordered.

"Wait a minute! What the hell do I know about delivering a baby?"

"You don't have to know anything; I'm the one that has to do all the work," Melinda said. "Now get your ass over here!"

Dr. Jason McQuaid was beginning to look worried.

"Now, Melinda, I know we've known each other since grade school, and I know I haven't always been nice to you, but you need to put those things aside and think about the baby. I was just kidding a little while ago. I'd love to look at your..."

Melinda threw her purse at him. "Pervert! T.D., get over here."

Georgia shoved me toward Melinda, and followed to get her by the arm and help her up onto a table.

I waited helplessly, but Jason grabbed me by the arm and steered me toward the kitchen. "At least wash your hands," he said.

He shoved me into the kitchen and instructed me to scrub all the way to my elbows with the vegetable brush on the sink. Cindy had disappeared into some other part of the basement, so I took the opportunity to probe Jason.

"I know you two hated each other in high school, but don't you think you're a little old for that now?"

"I do, but you know old habits are hard to break."

"What did you do to piss her off so bad?" I asked.

"You know the reputation she had in high school?"

"Who didn't? I mean, the whole gym class caught her in the showers with Ricky Pease."

"Well, apparently Ricky asked a little more smoothly than I did," Jason said.

"What do you mean?"

"You know how she said she wouldn't let me see it for free in high school?"

"You didn't."

He shrugged. "I wanted to be a gynecologist even back then."

I finished scrubbing and Jason grabbed a wad of paper towels from the rack.

"Now get in there and play doctor," he said.

By the time we got back in the other room, Melinda was already naked from the waist down and draped in a tablecloth. Georgia held her hand, and Melinda directed me to the foot of the table.

"Lift up the cloth and tell me what you see," she panted.

I'm sure I blushed because Georgia giggled in spite of herself.

Dutifully, I lifted the sheet.

"I see a butt," I said.

Melinda screamed again. "No shit. What else do you see?"

"No, I mean I see two butts," I said, panicking.

Jason shoved me out of the way, suddenly stone sober and giving more than a passing impersonation of a real, honest-to-God doctor.

"Get him away from me," Melinda screamed.

"The baby's breech, and either I deliver it or you lose it. So shut the hell up and do like I tell you to," he snapped.

The next thirty minutes were a blur. Jason would massage Melinda belly for a while, stick his arm under the cloth, and then massage some more. Finally, he gave her the okay to push, and in less than a minute he was holding a wriggling, screaming mass of bloody something that he said was a girl.

You couldn't prove it by me.

He laid the baby on Melinda's chest and assured her it was all right.

"We'll still need an ambulance pretty soon, though, to take you both to the hospital," he said.

"Thank you, Doctor," she said, turning her attention back to the baby, cooing and cuddling it.

Jason looked mildly surprised, but smiled in spite of himself as he turned back to me and Georgia.

"T.D, not many people would step up to try to do that. My hat's off to you." He stretched his hand out.

"Uh, thanks, but I'll wait 'till you wash up, if it's all right," I said.

Jason laughed. "If I have to wash first, I'm giving you a big, sloppy kiss instead of a handshake."

I took a step back quickly. "I better get out of here and check on the storm damage."

Georgia and I stepped out of the basement and into a considerably cooler afternoon than we had seen when we came in.

"T.D., you never cease to amaze me," Georgia said, hugging my arm. "You would have gone right ahead and done your best to deliver that baby if the doctor hadn't stepped in."

I didn't want to say, "Somebody had to," or "Anybody would have done the same thing," or any other cliché, so I just said nothing.

"You'll do just fine in the delivery room when we have a baby," she said.

My heart skipped a beat. "You never can tell; I might forget about this by then. That's still a looooong way away."

Georgia smiled a disconcerting smile.

"Not as long as you might think," she said. "Let's stop by the Dairy Queen. I'm hungry again."

PART TWELVE

THE PEPPERMINT TWISTER

ew things can leave your head spinning like a tornado. Finding out you're
going to be a father is one of them.

Georgia and I had no more than left the shelter in the basement of the
Presbyterian Church than she sprang the news on me, and in the wake of
Wakefield's first tornado in twenty years.

I might be the owner/publisher/editor of *The Wakefield Journal*, but that
doesn't mean I can blow off covering a tornado.

"T.D. Duff! I just told you I'm pregnant and you're going to run off on a
story?"

"Look, Georgia, we haven't had a tornado here since I was in elementary
school. I can't ignore it. Besides, if I'm going to be a daddy, I have to keep the
money coming in."

Georgia stuck out her lovely lower lip, but she couldn't argue with that
logic. I kissed her and let her out of the car in front of Van Hoose, Van Hoose,
and Vanderpool.

"I'll see you tonight," I said. "Let me know what the doctor says."

I drove away relieved that I had seen no damage so far, but still fretting
over my impending fatherhood. Georgia's first home pregnancy test had shown
a positive two nights before, and she had done two more to confirm it. She was
on her way to her regular doctor today to be referred to Jason McQuaid, the
local obstetrician, to get started on whatever regimen a pregnant woman had
to follow.

The Wakefield Journal's storefront office was undamaged when I pulled up in
front and ran in for my camera. Anabelle, my long-suffering receptionist, was
quaking with excitement when I walked through the front door.

"Yes, Anabelle, I know there was a tornado," I said.

"No kidding. I figured you knew that, but did you hear anything else exciting while you were out?"

"Well, I helped deliver a baby for Melinda Creech," I said, expecting another explosion of excitement.

"You did not. You just watched while Doc McQuaid delivered it."

I had left the shelter only fifteen minutes earlier. News travels fast around Augusta County.

"How did you know that?"

"My sister Pam's husband, Roy, has a cousin Elizabeth whose sister-in-law Karen is a Presbyterian. The pastor's wife told her friend Rebecca, who told Plumber Tom's wife, Donna, and she told Karen. Well, of course Karen can't keep a secret about anything so she called Elizabeth while she and Pam were over at the Hair Port getting perms."

"Sorry I asked."

"You should be. I'm talking about the baby anyway. Not that one, I mean."

I stumbled as I started through the hallway toward my office.

"How did you...? Oh, the pastor's wife and the brother-in-law of the cousin of the sister?"

"It's the sister-in-law of the cousin, and, no, of course not. Georgia called me to make sure you weren't upset."

I tried to keep the eye-rolling in control.

"I'm not upset. I'm happy. Really. Now, let's drop it. I've gotta find out about storm damage."

"Peppermint Meadows," Anabelle said suddenly, grabbing a phone message slip off her desk and handing it over.

I read the message as I started for the door.

"Four homes a total loss, three cars damaged, wow! Where is Peppermint Meadows? I thought I knew every place in Augusta County."

"It's the old Shaller farm. The kids subdivided it."

"You mean the trailer park on the east end of town?"

"That's it."

"That figures."

I drove out of town past the Southern States store, past the Ford dealership's Big Columbus Day Tent Sale, and past rickety old coal camp houses falling into the street. All of them were untouched by the tornado. But when I turned on Highway 62, I was greeted by a highway littered with bits of insulation, strips of vinyl siding, shingles, and a La-Z-Boy recliner sitting in the middle of the two-lane.

I maneuvered around the chair, turned left on Peppermint Avenue, and saw the source of the detritus. The tornado had dipped in over a brick house beside the trailer park, wiped out a whole row of mobile homes, then skipped back over a hundred-year-old farmhouse on the other end. The only damages to the adjoining properties were some splintered tree tops and a piece of bent roofing tin on the farmhouse.

I turned left again on Julep Drive and stopped on the edge of the gravel road. A chunky man in a John Deere hat and flannel shirt sat on the tailgate of a badly damaged Ford pickup, smoking a cigar and staring at the remains of a trailer.

"Howdy!" I called as I approached.

The man waved half-heartedly over his shoulder and never turned around.

I walked over with my camera and joined him on the tailgate.

"I'm T.D. Duff from *The Wakefield Journal*. That yours?"

"Was," he said shortly, nodding to acknowledge my introduction. "Bob Miller."

He stuck out his hand. I shook it and expressed my sympathy the best I could.

"Jeez, too bad, Bob. It's a real wreck."

"Yep. Third trailer I've lost."

"You're kidding. Tornadoes get the other two?"

"Ex-wives. Same thing."

I snapped some pictures and took some notes while I talked to Bob about his plight. He had taken the worst of the damage at Peppermint Meadows. One of the other three trailers had burned a month earlier and two others were vacant rentals.

I was finishing up with him when Anabelle called. More damages had been reported on McAllister Road and at another trailer park near Falls River.

Since I already had pictures of destroyed trailers, I went to McAllister Road first. Sure enough: more trailers.

Augusta County Emergency Management Chief Wilbur Ross was chewing tobacco and spitting out the window of his Tahoe when I climbed into the passenger seat.

"Afternoon, Sparky," I said, using the nickname the chief preferred to answer to.

"'Lo, T.D. Gettin' any good pictures?"

"I thought so, but I can only use so many shots of ripped-up trailers. Is there anything else damaged?"

"You kiddin'? It was tornadoes that hit. What else they gonna tear up?"

Sparky wasn't helpful.

"Surely there's a roof torn off somewhere or a car turned over or something."

"Nope. Just trailers."

I trudged back to the road and drove back to Wakefield. With the tornado coverage behind me, I had time to think about Georgia and me and the baby. The deadline wasn't for another four days for next week's edition, so I had plenty of time. I left the office at five and drove toward Georgia's house. I had only one stop to make on the way.

It was dark inside when she opened the door after the second knock. She walked silently to the living room, leaving the door for me to close.

When I turned the light on as I entered, the glowing, smiling Georgia I expected wasn't there. She looked more dejected and sad than I had ever seen her. Tears streaked both cheeks, and her lower lip quivered. I felt my own heart drop into my stomach.

"What's wrong?"

"The home pregnancy tests," she said. "I'm not having a baby."

To my surprise, the news didn't raise my spirits. Rather than a great weight being lifted from my shoulders, I felt as though another hundred-pound sack of corn had been added. I had thought I would be happy if she had never told me I was going to be a father. From her puzzled look, she apparently thought so, too.

"You're not happy?"

"Oddly enough, no. I'm not."

"The way you reacted when I told you I was pregnant, I thought you'd be ecstatic."

"So did I."

"Well, I'm glad you're sad."

I had to chuckle at the sentiment.

"I mean…you know what I mean. I wish I could do something to make you feel better," she said.

"Oh, you can."

Georgia groaned. "Men! Let me see if I can guess."

I pulled the ring box out of my jacket pocket and held it out to her.

"See if you can guess now."

PART THIRTEEN

A WEDDING IN WAKEFIELD

Danny Vaughn hung up the phone and grinned an evil grin at Larry Stone and Kyle Pelphry.

"It's all set up. Georgia and Joy have got two friends from their modeling days who will be coming in for the wedding, and they don't mind doing a bachelor party at all."

Kyle frowned doubtfully. "I don't know, man. Having the bridesmaids strip for the bachelor party is just weird."

"There's only the two of them," Danny said. "And weird is great. T.D. will shit."

Larry grinned in spite of himself.

"He will do that."

Kyle glared at him and Larry wiped the smile off his face. "Still, Kyle's right. I mean, they're Georgia's best friends. T.D.'s going to be too embarrassed to have a good time."

"Oh, he'll get over it," Danny said.

The bell over the funeral home's front door rang, and a moment later T.D. came into the room. Dressed in blue jeans, an open-collared dress shirt, tweed jacket, and open wool overcoat, T.D. looked the part of a rumpled newspaperman.

He pulled his notebook out of his hip pocket and tossed it on the desk before he flopped down in a chair.

"Man, it's good to have a break, even if it is with y'all," he said.

"Tough day at the office, Mr. Hurst?" Kyle asked.

"Tough ain't the half of it," T.D. said. "The tornado three months ago, then nothing through Thanksgiving, Christmas, and New Year's, and now I can't get time to breathe."

"Well, 'tis the season for car wrecks, falls, and plane crashes," Larry said. "I've done more X-rays than normal, too."

"Yeah, but who would expect two plane crashes in a week? In Augusta County, no less."

"Well, the one don't count. Anybody that would fly an open ultralight in January ought to crash," Danny said.

"You're just mad because he didn't have the courtesy to die so you'd get some business," Larry accused.

"I don't want any more business, thank you," Danny said. "I need time to plan a bachelor party and a wedding. Besides, do you know how hard it is to dig when the ground's this frozen?"

T.D. grimaced. "Look, guys, no bachelor party. I don't have time, and I don't want to be driving two hours to a strip club the night before my wedding."

"Who said anything about driving? I've reserved a suite at the Travelodge right here in Wakefield," Danny said.

T.D. groaned. Kyle looked shocked. "They have suites at the Travelodge?"

"And Jacuzzis," Danny said.

"Guys, let's nip this in the…" T.D.'s pager interrupted him. "Crap, there's a shootout on Old Taylor Road."

"In Augusta County???" Danny asked.

"You got it." T.D. stood up and headed for the door. "First time I've ever heard of a gunfight around here."

"Keep your head down," Larry advised.

Kyle stood up and hitched up his gun belt. "Guess I better go, too."

"You're a game warden. Unless it's an irate deer taking its revenge, what are you gonna do?" Larry asked.

"I'm a sworn peace officer," Kyle said. "If there's a crime in progress, I'm obligated to try and stop it."

"If you say so, Barney," Danny said.

Larry stood up, too, and pulled his coat on over his scrubs. "Guess they might need me at the hospital."

Danny took his own suit coat off and started for the basement door. "If you all are that excited, I guess I better straighten out the embalming room, just in case."

"Ghoul," Larry said as he started out.

"Quack," Danny shot back.

Both the sheriff's deputies and Willie Roark missed what they were shooting at, so Danny's services weren't needed for the day. Larry did have to X-ray the ankle of a T.V. reporter who fell off her high heels on the ice outside Roark's hillside marijuana grow house. T.D. got a story and pictures out of the incident, including one of the reporter with her skirt over her head as she lay in snow at the foot of the hill.

"Who would've thought she was wearing sweatpants under that?" Danny said, marveling at the photo.

"Well, it was pretty cold and windy. I guess a dress would have been sort of uncomfortable without sweats," Kyle replied.

Danny looked at his watch. "Three hours 'til the rehearsal dinner, then it's off to the bachelor party. You buy the beer?"

"I got it and I hid it from Larry."

"You're a good man. I've got him over at the hotel decorating the room."

"Good. What about the girls?"

"They'll be at the rehearsal dinner, then they'll come right over."

"Sure does seem strange, having the women there, too."

"It's only the outta-towners," Danny said. "It's not like Georgia's gonna be there."

Georgia checked her watch for the umpteenth time. It was six-twenty and T.D. should have been at the church at six sharp. The Rev. Cecil Nelson sat on the stage, staring at the ceiling and twiddling his thumbs. The groomsmen were huddled in the corner laughing and casting furtive glances at the bridesmaids, who lounged seductively on the left front pew.

Joy was the exception. She sat backwards on a chair positioned at the front window, her nose pressed against the glass as she gave a play-by-play of what was happening outside.

"Here comes a red pickup. Nope, it's a Dodge. Not him. Man, the snow is really coming down now. I thought the South was supposed to be warm. There's something else red. It's a car. Sorry. Could he be driving anything else? Maybe the delivery van? Oh, wait! Here he comes. He's...nope. Not him. I wonder..."

"Joy, shut up," Georgia said. "He'll be here when he gets here. I knew he was going to be late as soon as I heard all those sirens."

Joy started to say something, but instead made the "tick-a-lock" gesture on her lips, got up from the window, and scurried to the front of the room to talk to the other bridesmaids, who were still having a ball tormenting the groomsmen.

Georgia was checking her watch again when T.D. burst through the back door of the church.

"Sorry I'm late. I tried to get here, I swear," he said.

"Yeah, yeah," Georgia said. "We heard the sirens and knew you'd be chasing an ambulance."

"Actually, no one was hurt, so it wasn't an ambulance; it was a fire truck— bunches of fire trucks. You see, the..."

"T.D.?" Georgia interrupted, "I. Don't. Care. I wanna practice the wedding, have the rehearsal dinner, and go home. The wedding's tomorrow."

"Don't worry, honey, everything will be all right," T.D. said.

Danny dragged him to the altar as Georgia and her attendants went into the anteroom at the front of the church to prepare. Since Georgia's parents were dead, Van Hoose, Sr., the senior partner at Van Hoose, Van Hoose, and Vanderpool, was going to give her away. He followed the four former models into the anteroom with a huge smile on his face, winking at the groomsmen as he ducked out the door.

The rehearsal went off without a hitch other than Georgia head-butting the reverend when she dropped her bouquet and they both bent to get it at the same time. As soon as his nose stopped bleeding, he continued with the rehearsal.

"I dow prodouth you huthbad ad wife," the reverend said around the tissue packed in his nostrils. "You bay kiss."

T.D. leaned in, but Danny grabbed him by the elbow.

"Come on, we gotta get this rehearsal dinner done. Remember, we've got other things to do."

T.D. had reserved the back dining room at the Red Bull for the dinner, a short five-minute drive from the church. Kyle and Larry rode in Danny's car, which turned it into a three-minute drive with Larry rolling around in the back as Danny took the curves faster than a hearse was meant to travel.

"Damn it, Danny, I don't wanna be riding in the back of one of these things for real. Slow the hell down," Larry griped.

"Are you kidding me? Did you see those bridesmaids? The bachelor party is waiting, and the sooner we get this dinner over with, the sooner we can get started on the real fun."

T.D. and Georgia were somewhat slower arriving and were content to sit quietly and enjoy the prime rib. Allie and Ronni, the bridesmaids, ate small salads and excused themselves quickly. Ronni took the hotel key from Danny and slipped it into her push-up bra.

"Aren't you girls going to eat any more than that?"

"We don't want to be all bloated," Allie explained with a wink at Ronni.

"T.D., you ready to go?" Larry asked quickly.

"No, I'm not," T.D. said.

"Of course he's not," Mama Duff scolded. "He's not even finished with his steak."

"He needs to watch what he eats anyway. Didn't he tell you about his cholesterol?" Danny asked her, taking T.D. by the arm.

"What about it? T.D., have you been keeping something from me?"

"No, Mama, my cholesterol is fine," he protested as Kyle got his other arm and pulled him up from the table.

"Now, T.D., be honest with your mother," Larry said. "You know I work at the hospital and I'm not supposed to say anything, but T.D. really needs to tell you himself. In the meantime, no more steak."

He held the door open as Kyle and Danny dragged T.D. out.

"Let me go! I can make it to the bachelor party on my own!"

"The question isn't if you'll make it, it's when," Danny said, "and we can't start without the guest of honor. That means we're getting you there quick if we have to tie you to the roof of the car. Kyle, you drive T.D.'s truck."

T.D. sat in the passenger seat of his own truck as Kyle followed the hearse to the hotel.

The valet hesitated when Danny reached out to him with the key, but he finally took it, trying to look through the tinted back glass of the Caddy before getting in.

"Don't worry...if there's anybody back there, they're not going to complain about your driving," Danny told him.

Kyle and Danny whisked T.D. through the lobby and up the stairs to the second floor while Larry ran ahead to open the door. He already had a beer in each hand by the time the rest of them got to the room.

"T.D, it's time you had a beer and relaxed a little," Larry said, expertly cracking open a can with one hand, and turning it up to his lips.

"Thanks, Lar." T.D. reached for the other can, but Larry had already finished the first one and was opening the second.

"Get your own, buddy boy," he said, turning up the second brew.

"You're gonna be blind drunk before the girls come in," Kyle warned.

Larry drained the second can and tossed it into the trash can.

"Good. That'll give me an excuse when Hilda finds out. I was kidnapped. And drunk."

T.D. started to the cooler when a bass beat swelled from the speakers, the door to the second room of the suite flew open, and the two bridesmaids pranced out wearing the stripper equivalent of bridal costumes.

Ronni pushed T.D. into a chair and began dancing in front of him while Allie worked her way behind the chair and leaned over to kiss his ear.

Larry drank another beer and whooped at the top of his lungs. Danny and Kyle grinned as T.D. protested the show by his bride-to-be's best friends.

The song stopped and the two girls struck a pose while the next one began. The next music anyone heard, however, was T.D.'s pager.

He sprang out of his chair and backed toward the door, pulling the pager from his belt as he did.

"Crap! I gotta go. I'll see you all tomorrow. Bye!"

He ran out the door and slammed it shut.

"We were just getting started!" Allie protested.

"That's okay, girls, we're still here," Kyle said, bouncing into T.D.'s chair. "You can pick up right where you left off."

❧

Ronni took off her sunglasses and eyed the mirror critically.

"I don't look half bad, considering the hangover I've got." She turned to Georgia. "On the other hand, girl, you look like hell."

"Gee, thanks. That's what every woman wants to hear on her wedding day," Georgia snapped.

"It's worry," Ronni said. "I mean, you look beautiful, but you got your forehead all wrinkled up like a prune. You gotta relax, girl."

"It's three minutes 'til the ceremony is supposed to start and T.D.'s still not here. How can I relax? And, by the way, maybe he would be on time if it wasn't for you and Allie."

"Don't blame us," Allie said. "I told you already, T.D. got a page five minutes after he got there and took off like a rocket. You don't have to worry about him stepping out on you unless he's stepping out to work. Ronni practically suffocated the boy in her boobs and he was trying to get away."

Joy popped into the room, adjusting her blue maid-of-honor gown as she did.

"Are you ready to go?" she asked brightly.

"Is T.D. here?" Georgia replied.

"Not yet."

"Then there you are. No, I'm not ready to go."

Someone knocked at the door, and Joy opened it. Van Hoose, Sr. stood outside nervously, trying to see around her.

"Is everybody decent?"

"Hell, honey, we're better than that," Ronni said, straightening the top of her thigh-high.

"Come in, Van. We're just waiting for T.D.," Georgia said, tugging Ronni's dress back down.

"I just saw him pull in; that's why I came back here," Van said.

"See, I told you he'd be here," Joy told her.

Two seconds later, Danny knocked on the door and stuck his head in without waiting for an invitation.

"Groom's here. Are you ready to go?"

"We're ready. Line up," Joy ordered the others. "Tell the pianist she can start."

Danny gave a thumbs-up toward the front of the church and the procession began.

T.D. stood at the altar and watched as the groomsmen and the bridesmaids made their way up the aisle. Finally, the pianist performed her dramatic bridge from "The Wedding Song" to "The Bridal March," and Georgia stepped through the back door on Van Hoose, Sr.'s arm. His heart jumped, partly from her beauty and partly from his fear that she was going to step on the gown and cause someone bodily injury. His fears turned out to be unfounded, as Georgia made it to the front of the church without hurting anybody.

"Who gives this woman to be wed?" the Rev. Nelson asked, his voice barely impeded by the bandage on his nose.

"On behalf of her parents, I do," Van Hoose, Sr. intoned.

And so the wedding proceeded with "I wills" and "I dos," until the pastor finally gave his permission for them to kiss.

T.D. lifted her veil just as pagers sounded all over the church. Sheriff Charlie Stewart, a deputy, and four members of the Wakefield Volunteer Fire Department immediately got up and walked hurriedly to the back door. T.D. grabbed for his own pager, but he was too slow. Georgia already had it. She pushed the button to silence it and tossed it over T.D.'s head to Danny.

"Ladies and gentlemen," Georgia said, "I regret to tell you that T.D. and I will not be able to attend the reception. We're going on our honeymoon. Now."

She grabbed T.D. by the arm and dragged him down the aisle and out the door as the pianist tried vainly to keep up with their pace.

Larry craned his neck to see over Danny's shoulder as he checked the pager.

"What happened?"

"Courthouse is on fire," Danny said. "Guess T.D. will just have to read about it in the paper."

"Who's gonna put it in? He's gone on his honeymoon."

Danny clipped the pager to his belt.

"If I can embalm a body and make it look like they're just sleeping, I guess I can breathe some life into that old rag, too," he said. "I always thought he needed a Page Three Girl like those papers over in England have. What do you guys think?"

ABOUT THE AUTHOR

Sam Adams is a freelance writer, and former newspaper reporter, photographer and editor. A native of Appalachia, he lives in rural eastern Kentucky with his wife and three children.

He is the author of *Precious Blood* (2007, Pinnacle Books), and hundreds of non-fiction articles on subjects such as crime, the environment, politics, healthcare and outlandish vegetables.